Anancy Mek It

Bedtime Stories from Jamaica

Peter-Paul Zahl

LMH Publishing Limited

Cover Layout: Susan Lee-Quee

Anancy Concept & Cover Illustration: Christian Hansen

Text Illustrations: Steve Thomas

Book Design, Layout & Typeset: Michelle M. Mitchell

Published by: LMH Publishing Limited
7 Norman Road,
LOJ Industrial Complex,
Building 10,
Kingston C.S.O., Jamaica.
Tel: 876-938-0005; 938-0712
Fax: 876-759-8752
Email: lmhbookpublishing@cwjamaica.com
Website: www.lmhpublishingjamaica.com

Printed in the U.S.A.   ISBN: 976-8184-34-5

Dedicated to Alex and Juan Ramon

Contents

How Anancy Stories Came About

Once upon a time when tigers and lions went on their hindlegs, wasps had teeth, mongoose ate vegetables, pigs had small mouths, snakes lived in palaces, owls flew around in bright daylight wearing sunglasses, Jamaica's national dish was toast-bread with butter and jam, fire was living in the bush, and mosquitoes used to talk, there was a charming little trickster who was always lazy, hungry and sly. He lived in a small village in the country, and his name was Anancy.

One night when he was walking on the road he passed an old woman's yard. She sat in a rocking chair on the verandah and read a story out of a big, fat book. She was surrounded by her grand-children. Well, Anancy always is curious. So he hid behind a tree near to the verandah and listened. The granny read, the children listened, laughed and shuddered with big eyes and only watched Granny's lips.

Anancy tiptoed nearer and had a look at the book. He saw a picture of a young girl with a red hood.

"But koo-yah! One likkle fool-fool gal wid a red ridin' hood an one basket wid bread an wine ina book. Wha 'bout me? Me nuh ina de book?"

The granny turned the page: No picture of Anancy. He

got vexed, went home, ate a piece of roast' yam with butter, and went to bed. He still was thinking about the book. Next morning he passed a kindergarten. There a young Miss sat on a hammock, swinging back and forth, holding a magazine in her hands and reading aloud for some children gathered around.

"But see-yah, what an excitement!" Anancy wondered.

The children laughed, clapped hands, gave each other a punch in the ribs, and had shining eyes.

Anancy tiptoed around, stepped behind the young woman and peeped into the magazine.

"Lawwwwdamassi!" he exclaimed. "One fool-fool magazine wid some ducks in a it. One big one an t'ree likkle ones. Me wonda wedda one picture wid me inna de book."

But whenever the young lady turned the pages he didn't see any picture of himself.

"Outa order biznis dat," Anancy thought, "de book dem hav all kinda pictures! An' no story wid me an' no picture show fi me pretty face! Firs some eediat ducks an den one fool-fool mouse name' Micky. Ongly animals dat hav no sense atall-atall! An wha happen to di pickney-dem? Dem hav no sense. It look like dem like dem kinda stories. Dat haffi change!"

In those days, the cat and the mouse used to be good friends. Every day they played together and had lots of fun when they could steal things. Yes, they were robbers and thieves! They respected nobody. Everybody fell victim to them. Where ever cat and mouse saw a piece of meat or cheese, a cob of corn, a chicken-leg, sausages, ham, salami or a saucer with milk they had to go there and steal. When a door or window was open, Brer Puss sneaked inside and stole some food. Whenever the door was closed or a window only slightly open, and Brer Puss could not press through, his friend Brer Rat sneaked into the room and t'ieved for himself and his best friend. Both of them were notorious thieves. Even Anancy had been a victim several times, so his mother asked him to catch and kill them to stop this crime, and the worst was that Anancy and his mother were poor and sometimes didn't have anything to eat!

So one day Brer Anancy sitting down in his armchair, smoking a pipe began to think of finding a solution. After a while he got up. He had an idea...

The next morning he passed the ball-ground. He could see how Brer Puss and Brer Rat were enjoying themselves playing hopscotch, hide-and-seek and catch-me-if-you can. They were looking happy. Anancy hid behind a tree, watching. It wasn't long after he saw the friends part to stroll to their yards to have lunch.

Fast like lightning Anancy took a shortcut to reach the road that was leading to Brer Puss yard before him. He patiently waited for the cat.

"Good day, good day, Brer Puss," he said when the cat was approaching him.

Brer Puss raised his tail and watched him cautiously. As he had no manners he neither said "Howdy!" nor "Meow!"

"But Brer Puss me nah unnerstan yuh," Anancy said slowly.

Bewildered the cat stopped in his tracks.

"How yuh mean?" he purred.

"How come," Anancy continued, "seh yuh an Brer Rat play wid each adda day in an day out?"

"How yuh mean?" asked Brer Puss.

"Well, me wonda why yuh play wid him an...nuh nyam him."

"Nyam him?" Brer Puss whispered. His eyes got bigger and bigger.

"Nyam him!" Anancy nodded. "Yuh nebba evva tase rat-meat yet?"

Anancy licked his lips. "Dat a real delicacy," he said firmly. "Suppen fi rich people wid a good taste. Yuh nuh even try i' yet?"

"Smaddy can eat rat?" Brer Puss wondered.

"Yeah, man," Anancy declared, "rat-meat betta dan ham!"

"Betta dan ham?" whispered Brer Puss and licked his mouth. "Ah true?"

"True, true," Anancy said hypocritically.

Brer Puss licked his mouth again, bade Anancy a friendly farewell, and moved in a straight line to his yard.

Anancy grinned and ran to the mouse's yard. He knocked on the door. Brer Rat opened it cautiously.

"Bad news!" Anancy cried. "Bad news fi true!"

He pretended to be out of breath.

"Wha happen?" Brer Rat squeakily asked.

"Me hear suppn terrible!" Anancy whispered.

"Dat ah what?" Brer Rat breathed terrified. "Tell me right now, fast-fas!"

"Jus' imagine," Anancy slowly told him, "me jussa pass Brer Puss yard an den me hear..."

"Ah wha yu hear?" shrieked Brer Rat.

"Well, me hear how Madda Puss tell fi har likkle one..."

"Wha him tell fi me frien'?"

"Madda Puss did tell fi yuh frien' kitten seh him nuh

4

suppose fi play wid rat."

"Not fi play wid me?" Brer Rat said bewildered.

"Wussera dan dat!" Anancy shouted. And he continued cautiously: "Madda Puss tell fi him yout fi catch ebbry rat an fi kill him an fi nyam him causen rat-meat nicerer dan ham!"

Brer Rat closed his eyes. The ground seemed to shake

beneath his feet. He nearly fainted.

"T'anks," he finally said. "T'anks fi warn me! Yuh's a real good frien'!"

And he turned fast like lightning and closed his door, turned the key twice, and slammed the windows shut.

Anancy smiled and went home.

From that day, mice and rats hide whenever they hear or see or smell a cat. And from that day cats are hunting down rats and mice. They are so deadly in this hide-and-seek that the two of them barely have any time left to thieve other people.

Anancy mek it

Well, one day the humans and animals found out that it had been Anancy who turned cats and rats into enemies. And one day an old lady said to him. "Brer Anancy, we unnerstan' seh it was yuh who turn' dese dangerous thieves into enemies for life. Ebbrybaddy say t'anks. Yes, we's so grateful seh yuh can aks fi anything we can do fi yuh. Yuh hav any wish?"

"Oh yes," Anancy said. "Me did see seh inna alla di pickney books an magazines all kinda story-dem bout rat and puss an lion an mermaids an riding-hoods an ducks. An all ah dem juss boast so. It is a disgrace! An me... me is not in one ah de book dem. Not one picture! Not one story! It's a shame!"

After a while of good thinking the old lady said: "Well, Anancy, nuh worry. Dat sekkle. From now on me an alla de adda ole woman-dem an fadas and maddas gwaan tell stories 'bout yuh ebbry night fi de pickney-dem. Awrite?"

Anancy bowed. He got tears in his eyes. He smiled. He walked to his yard like in a dream.

But to be frank: He does not trust big people. No way!

That was the reason why he used to control whether the old lady told the truth. Whenever a mother or a father or a helper or a granny or a nurse or a teacher tells bedtime stories to children, Anancy turns into a spider and hides in a corner of the ceiling and listens. If somebody forgets to tell an Anancy-story to a child who has brushed his teeth, has wiped off good-good or took a shower or bath, Anancy slides down a spider's thread and shows himself to the

grown-up person. And whenever this person starts to doze off and the pickney still is half-awake, Anancy puts a part of the cobweb over the person's face and wakes him or her up. Then this big person tells an Anancy-story, and the pickneys tell Anancy-stories to other pickneys, and they tell and tell and tell till everybody tells an Anancy-story.

Anancy mek it.

Jack Mandora, me nuh choose none.

Anancy and Tiger

Once upon a time Tiger was a good looking fellow. He wore a three piece suit and a hat; when he walked down the road on his two muscular legs, he used to spin his walking stick elegantly and to flirt with every pretty girl. There was only one guy who was more handsome and vainer than Tiger, and that was Brer Peacock. But Tiger was stronger than everybody, accept for Brer Elephant and Brer Lion who were both stronger, and people still guessed whether Brer Jaguar was weaker or stronger than Tiger.

The only person who did not have any respect for Tiger was Anancy. But he did not show this because he knew Tiger might hurt him. He and Tiger had fallen in love with the same girl. She was the prettiest girl in the district. Even Brer Coney who lived in his hole and was half-blind had fallen in love with this girl. Brer Pattoo a.k.a. Owl who always flew around with his darkers in bright daylight was full of praise of her. These fellows were no competition for Anancy, but Brer Tiger...

Well, Anancy lay down in his hammock, lit his pipe, and racked his brain. The next morning, he waited until Tiger had gone to the gymn to do his body-building, and then walked to Serena's yard – this was the name of the girl.

So Serena asked him pityfully: "Wha happen, Anancy? Me nevva see yuh so sad."

"Woiiii!" Anancy sighed. "Me simply nuh unnerstan yuh."

"Yuh nuh unnerstan me? Wha wrong wid me, Anancy?"

"Wha wrong wid yu?" Anancy cried, and because he was so excited he got a lisp. "Why yuh athociate wid Tiger?

Him of all people! Him, is fi me faada'th ole riding horthe!"

"Fi yuh faada's old riding-horse?" Serena cried.

"Yeth, man," Anancy nodded, "de subthtitute fa da jackath! Tiger, de good-fa-nuttin! Him who cyaan carry de two bankra dem pon him back. De ongly ting him good at ith boathting."

Serena showed her disgust. "Yuh's absolutely right, Nancy," she shouted, "him's bad company fi true."

Anancy suppressed a smile, and bade Serena goodbye.

An hour later, Tiger approached Serena's yard. He had taken a shower, put on sweet-smelling lotion and aftershave, his moustache was combed, he wore his Sunday's best and a hat, and gayly spinned his cane.

Serena watched him from head to toe in disgust, and turned away.

Brer Tiger was totally confused now. "Wha wrong wid yuh, Beautiful?" he said.

Serena took a short, arrogant look at him: "Excuse me, sah," she said after a short while, "me nuh socialise wid a former riding an pack animal!"

"Pack animal, me?" Tiger exclaimed. "Whose pack-animal?"

"Yuh's suppose fi know dat better dan me," Serena replied. "Anancy puppa former substitute fe de pack-mule."

"Anancy puppa... Ah who did tell yuh...?"

"Finally Anancy told me de trut' bout yuh," Serena coolly said. "An me's very grateful fi dat."

"Anancy a damned liad!" Brer Tiger shouted.

Serena watched him scornfully.

"An me gwaan prove i'!" Tiger roared. "Me gwaan kill him! But before dat, me gwaan drag him right yah so, an' him haffi tek back dat blastid slander!"

"Juss do wha yuh haffi do, sah," Serena spat. "Pack-animal-dem nuh have no manners. An de bes' proof ah dat ah de way how yuh juss shout 'bout so 'pon me verandah. No, Sir, me nuh wan have no dealings wid yuh again!"

Trembling with rage Tiger ran to Anancy's house. But Anancy was well prepared: He was lying in his bed, a wet piece of cloth on his forehead, he was covered with two thick sheets, and he moaned and groaned and sighed.

Tiger did not care at all: "Yuh haffi get up right now, Anancy," he shouted. "Yuh haffi come wid me to Serena yard, an yuh haffi tek back dat nasty lie yuh tell pon me!"

"Joke. A joke me ah mek," Anancy whispered wiping sweat from his face.

"Joke? Dat yuh ah call a joke?" Tiger roared. "De mos' nasty lie yuh tell pon me an now yuh haffi pay fi dat!"

"Do ath yuh like, Brer Tiger," Anancy moaned. "Me gwaan dead right now, an me cyaan get up at all."

"Me nuh give a damn wedda yuh sick or half-dead," Tiger shouted. "Yuh haffi come wid me, even if me haffi carry yuh to Serena yard."

"Awright, Brer Tiger," Anancy sighed, "dat ah de ongly way me can reach deh so."

Thus Tiger turned his back towards Anancy's bed, and Anancy tried to climb on Tiger's back. He tried it once, he tried it twice, he tried it four times, but always he'd slide down again. "Me ah go dead!" He moaned.

"Cho, man," Tiger hissed, "yuh haffi hold on firm on me neck or me shoulder."

"Me cyaan do dat, Brer Tiger. Me's juss too weak, sah. If yuh wan' seh me haffi reach Serena yard fi rectify de likkle joke, yuh haffi drop dong 'pon yuh two hand-dem an' walk four-legged. Me gwaan put a blanket pon yuh back, an..."

"'top de noise, Anancy," Tiger said. And he did what Anancy asked him to do. Anancy put a blanket on Tiger's back, climbed on it... and slid down deliberately.

"Noah, Brer Tiger, nuttin nuh go so," Anancy whispered. "Me's half dead awready, an me's too weak fi hold on yuh 'trong an' wide back. Two t'ings, only two tings me gwaan need..."

"Yuh a drive me crazy," Tiger roared, "Me gwaan kill yuh...!"

"But den me cyaan tek back de likkle joke me mek, Tiger. Is two tings me need..."

"Me know, me know," Tiger shouted, "do wha yuh wanna do, as long as yuh come wid me to Serena fi tek back yuh nasty lie."

Anancy was grinning now. But Tiger could not see this, as he was on his hands and feet and was looking forward.

"Me gwaan put suppen pon yuh de docta use fi call bridle, Brer Tiger, an den a pair ah stirrup fi put me weak foot-dem inna."

"Fi god's sake, Anancy," Tiger said, blind with rage, "put dat... idle pon me, an de blastid syrup, but come! Whole ah de worl' haffi hear seh Tiger's not a damd pack-mule."

Moaning and groaning Anancy put a saddle on Tiger's back, put on the bridle and his feet into the stirrups, and he jumped on Tiger's back. Very slowly and carefully Tiger now started to walk fourlegged. As soon as he had reached the threshold, Anancy grabbed the whip he had hidden on the door-frame, pressed his knees and feet against Tiger's sides thus forcing him to run. And Tiger ran!

Reaching Serena's frontyard, Anancy cracked the whip,

and he shouted: "Seen, Serena, me bring de livin proof seh Tiger ah nuttin but a stupid riding-harse!"

And cracking his whip and shouting "Geeho! Hoy!" he rode around in Serena's yard. Reaching the verandah he jumped from Tiger's back, bowed elegantly and smiled. Serena and all her neighbours now witnessed how Tiger was feeling shame, feeling shame, feeling shame! And as fast as lightning Tiger took to his heels feeling shame and rage.

From that day tigers walk on their four feet living in the jungle and not with people again.

Anancy mek it.

Jack Mandora, me nuh choose none.

Anancy and Ackee & Saltfish

Once upon a time Brer Saltfish was living in the sea. He was a very handsome fish. Everybody used to admire him. Thus Brer Saltfish got very vain and turned into a megalomaniac. He used to look down on everybody, did not listen to good advice anymore, and spent whole days in front of the mirror. Now he called himself *The Honourable Sir Cod.*

Well, pride comes before a fall. One day when Sir Cod was very hungry, he got careless and snapped for a worm which wiggled in front of him – and got hooked!

Anancy had caught him. Well, Anancy pulled the line with the hook and flung the big fish into his small boat. When he reached the shore, he salted the cod-fish and put him on a net to dry in the sun.

After a week or so a young girl sat on a boulder near to the net and looked into her little mirror to put lipstick on.

Sir Cod turned his head and looked into the girl's mirror. His eyes nearly popped out in horror.

"Whoiiiii, poor me," bawled Sir Cod, "how me tu'n ugly so? Me's so ugly no gal will marry me!"

At this moment Anancy turned up. He saw the fish bawling.

"Wha happen to yuh?" he asked Cod.

"Nobody nevva will love me," Sir Cod cried. "Me's so blastid ugly."

"But no," Anancy replied. "Yuh just...change a likkle bit. Yuh tu'n from Sir Cod into... *Duke Saltfish*. An yuh is the mos' handsome saltfish me see in me life. But me's sorry fi yuh. Yuh mus' lonely. Mek we fine a frien' fi yuh. Because yu know, even me nuh like so-so saltfish."

Brer Saltfish stopped bawling. "Yes, fine a good frien' fi me," he shouted.

The next morning Anancy introduced Sister Avocado Pear to Saltfish.

"Sen' har off, sen' har off!" cried Saltfish. "How yuh can t'ink seh me'll like har? She's so ugly!"

"Sista Avocado Pear ugly? Yuh mad! She a pretty, pretty gal!"

"Pretty?" Saltfish cried, "She ugly like! Juss look. She hav purple skin fulla warts."

"Him hav no manners," Anancy told Sister Avocado Pear. "Sorry fi de embarrassment."

"Dat awrite," Sister Pear said and walked away feeling embarrassed.

In the afternoon Anancy introduced Brer Cucumber to Saltfish.

"Seen?" he cried. "Me find a good frien' fi yuh."

"Friend?" Saltfish said scornfully. "Him ugly like. Juss look how him skin green. An him mawga so! No, Anancy, me nuh like him atall."

Before sunset Anancy carried Sister Papaya along and introduced her to Saltfish.

"No!" Saltfish shouted and turned up his nose. "Nuh introduce me to har! She look wicked an wile."

"Deh is no excuse fi him behaviour," Anancy said to Sister Papaya. "Me sorry!"

17

"Nuh badda, Brer Anancy," Sister Papaya replied politely, and walked off.

The whole evening and half the night, Anancy racked his brain. But the very moment before he fell asleep, he got an idea.

The next morning, he walked to the bush to find Sista Ackee.

He found her with all her sistren sitting in a tree.

"Yow!" Anancy cried. "Sista Ackee, howdy? Ebbryting awrite?"

"Yeah, man," Sista Ackee replied.

"Me unnerstan yuh got a new boyfrien', Sista Ackee. Ah true?"

"A joke, yuh ah joke," Ackee laughed. "No man. Me nuh wan' some so-so boyfriend! Me a look fi a good, good husban'."

"A husband?" Anancy cried. "Sista, me fine one fi yuh. A nice, nice fella. Sometimes him a likkle strange. But addawise him absolutely awrite. Hardworking, delicious, tough and sweet, same time..."

"Dat soun' good," Sista Ackee said. "Please, Anancy, do introduce me to him."

"Awrite," Anancy answered. So the two of them walked to the beach where Brer Saltfish lay on the net, taking a tan in the morning sun.

"Him look good fi true," Sista Ackee whispered, "But... Anancy, him smell so funny."

"Nuh worry, Sista Ackee," Anancy said. "Yuh nuh see him jus' get up. Him nuh bathe yet. Mek me soak him inna wata for a while, an me sure seh yuh an him will be bes' friends. No, no jus' friends. Oonoo haffi marry! Yuh an him mus' be husban' an wifey. Awrite?"

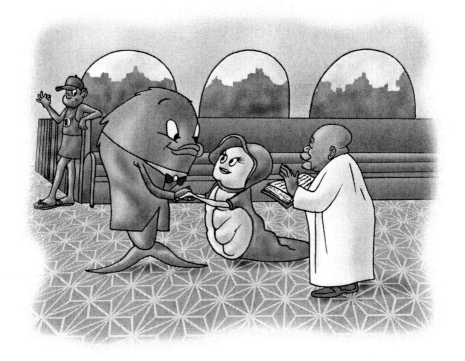

"Aks him now," Sista Ackee whispered. "Me's a likkle bit shy."

Well, Anancy ran to the next church and found a parson. And in the evening, there was a big, big wedding which took place on the beach.

From this day Ackee and Saltfish are married.

Anancy mek it.

Anancy and Rat

*L*ong time ago Brer Rat was an arrogant, facety, highfaluting and boasify guy. He was tremendously vain, cutting his moustache in a style, and he used to dress in the latest style and fashion. Yes, his boasting was hard to digest.

For a while Anancy tried to convince Brer Rat to change his ways. He pointed out to him that humans were more intelligent than he, tigers more dangerous, elephants bigger, parrots better dressed, flamingoes more elegant, owls wiser, black panthers more beautiful, and horses faster than rats.

But Brer Rat only laughed and insisted on being The Greatest.

So Anancy decided to cut Brer Rat to size. He sat down on his old, comfortable armchair, lighted his pipe, and racked his brain. It did not take him long to find out Brer Rat's weakness: He used to love to dance! He was a very good, no, a fantastic dancer! He went to every party, each bashment, to every dance. And when Brer Rat used to dance, for every bass and drum beat he invented a new step. Music and dance were things he could not resist at all.

Well, Anancy announced that he planned to have a big prize-dance. The best male dancer would get a crate of beer,

the best female dancer a food-basket. The whole district started practising the good, old folk-dances and the movements of the latest craze in the dancehalls. The dance would not be held in a bamboo-lawn but indoors in a very posh club. Admission was one hundred dollars, and lots of people complained. But then everybody saved their money to take part in the dancing contest. Anancy leased the club for the event and contracted a good band. He was confident that he would make a big bag of money out of this event. And he was even more confident that Brer Rat would turn up to win the first prize and that his, Anancy's plan to bring shame on Brer Rat would work out.

One hour before the club opened the gates for the dance, Anancy went inside, closed the door, turned the key two times – and fell to his knees. Not to pray but... to wax and shine the dancehall-floor until it was as slippery as ice. After that he told the band-leader his plan.

Well, the band opened the dance with lovely soft music, and the couples danced and spun slowly and in comfort. They waltzed and they foxtrotted and thought of the "good old days". After a while the music began getting faster. And Anancy was getting nervous because Brer Rat had not turned up yet. But then he realized that the real Dons and Rankin's and VIP's, in one word: People who thought they were more important than others always turned up later than the ordinary crowd. They wanted to be seen. And Anancy was sure now, that Brer Rat wanted to be seen bad-bad. Now the band started to play some good Old Hits – down the memory-lane – and the crowd just loved it. The dance-craze then was Ska. And Ska they now danced. Every man and every woman "shook foot" and had a very personal style to dance the Ska...

At last Brer Rat turned up. He wore the lates' in style and fashion. His two coloured shoes were pointed and made of suede. And his bell-bottom pants had seams as sharp as a razor-blade! He wore a cream-coloured silk-shirt with a wide-winged collar, and his cuff-links were of pure gold! In his back-pocket one could see the pretty, pretty rag to wipe his face.

Some couples even stopped dancing to admire him. Arrogantly Brer Rat pretended not to see the crowd. He lifted his left foot and started to dance. And how he danced! The rhythm went straight into his body and feet. He circled on one foot, he jumped up and down, he turned and twisted, he hopped, he crouched and squatted, he slowly, very slowly bent backwards and 'built a bridge', resting his body only on his fingertips and heels, jumped and got up again. Instead of one step on the beat, he made four steps, and he circled along the dancehall-floor in big speed. Everybody stopped dancing just to watch Brer Rat's movements and to shout: "Faster, Brer Rat, faster!" Or "Hey, hey, hey!"

But Brer Rat pretended to hear nothing. But now he even danced faster and faster.

Anancy grinned and gave the bandleader a sign. Now the band played an even faster tune. And Brer Rat spun on the spot and glided and tap-danced and was getting faster and faster, nearly as fast as a hurricane...

Anancy shook with laughter! – Brer Rat glided and glided and glided and glided as the dancehall-floor was as slippery as ice, and Brer Rat moved his arms like a windmill, and he started to stumble. And he began to slide even more, until suddenly his feet slid from under him and – BRA! BRAPS! – he landed on the floor on his backside.

First, there was a big silence, the band stopped, then laughter erupted. Every man and every woman started to laugh. And how they laughed! Some people tumbled down laughing. Others couldn't stop their tears, so hard were they laughing. Each and everybody laughed and pointed a finger at Brer Rat.

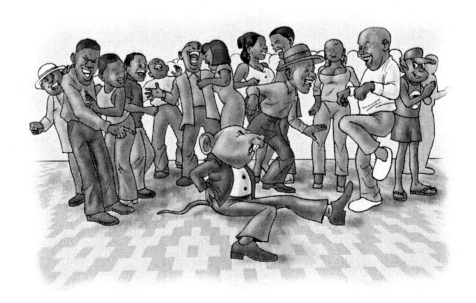

Brer Rat felt ashamed! Lawwwwwdamassi, he felt so ashamed!

He wished he was invisible! He wished the floor would open to hide him. He wished he could dissolve like gas in the air... All of a sudden, Brer Rat saw a hole in the wall of the dancehall. He ran to the hole, jumped into it – and disappeared.

All the dancers, the musicians and the people who only watched, everybody could not see him again!

From this day rats are living in holes.

Anancy mek it.

Jack Mandorah...

5

Anancy and Mosquito

nancy likes girls and women more than boys and men. "Ah so me stay," he use to say. "Me nuh know why, but in female company me juss feel better."

Well, he still had some good friends and brethren who had gone through thick and thin with him but whenever they were not around, he was attracted to women and girls. The only females he could not stand at all, were Sister Praying Mantis and Mrs. Scorpion, because they killed their husbands on their wedding night, and Miss Mosquita, because she liked to suck blood. But he liked Brer Mosquito who's called "Mass Masquito" by the small children. He was a handsome man with a nice moustache he used to stroke whenever he was in a deep conversation. And he was a vegetarian. Yes, male mosquitoes don't bite! They are good-mannered and nice.

Only sometimes Mass Mosquito got on Anancy's nerves.

Especially when he started to boast. And to be frank he really liked to show off and to boast. Lots of small people do that. What is missing in size they make up for with their big mouths.

But Anancy had a good heart. Whenever Mass Mosquito started to boast how much girlfriends he had, how much money was in the bank, and how much three-piece silk-suits were in his wardrobe, Anancy used to laugh inwardly and made a serious face and asked even more questions to find out how Mass Mosquito tried to worm his way out of his web of lies.

But one day Brer Mosquito really overdid it...

Once again he and Anancy were out of work. They had no food and no money. Thus they decided to "grab their cutlass", and started to farm. They got a bag full of yamheads and took over a piece of crownland in the bush.

So, while sharpening their machetes, Mass Mosquito talked about his father who, as he said, was one of the most successful yam-farmers around. Anancy only listened with half an ear. Sometimes he was sick and tired of his friend's boasting.

But Brer Mosquito did not notice that, and said: "Yes,

man, yuh can't imagine how big de yam-dem my faada used fi dig! One ah dem – me swear, Anancy! – did big like... did big like fi mi nose!"

"Fi yuh wha?" Anancy cried. "Repeat dat fi me!"

"Yah, man," his friend boasted, "him did dig out a White Yams as big as..."

"Fi yuh nose!" Anancy shouted and laughed.

"Mi nose, yes," Mosquito confirmed.

"Fi yuh... wha?" Anancy yelled.

Right now Mass Mosquito did not understand at all why Anancy was repeating his question several times, and he racked his brain and repeated: "Yes, juss like mi nose."

That moment, Anancy threw away his cutlass, and he jumped up laughing.

He put the file into his back-pocket, he grabbed his machete again, and jumped up and cried hysterically, giggling: "Fi yuh..."

"Noooossssssse!" Brer Mosquito stammered.

"Di whola di worl' muss hear dat," Anancy yelled.

And he ran to Brer Mongoose's house and told Brer Mongoose what Mass Mosquito had told him; and Brer Mongoose nearly dropped dead while laughing, and he laughed and coughed; and the two of them ran to Sister Yellow Snake's hole and told her about the size of the yam Brer Mosquito's father had reaped. Sister Yellow Snake wiggled with laughter; and then the three of them laughingly ran to Brer Monkey who was sitting on a branch of a guango-tree, and they shouted the story up to him, and Brer Anancy and his friends saw Monkey drop from the branch because he was laughing so hard; and the four of them ran to Brer Tiger in the jungle, and one after the other they told Brer Tiger about the huge yam Brer Mosquito's father

had dug, and Tiger twisted and turned, while laughing, and he was catching his tail so much he laughed and couldn't stop; and the five of them ran to Sister Fowl and told her about the extraordinary size of the yam Brer Mosquito's father had dug, and the corn Sister Fowl was chewing got stuck in her throat as she laughed so hard; and the six of them ran to Farmer Smith who was sitting on a bench under a breadfruit-tree in his yard, and they told him about the giant yam Mass Mosquito's father had dug, Farmer Smith burst out laughing, slapped his thighs, and ran into the kitchen to tell this story to his wife and seven children; and all of them ran into the village where Brer Elephant and his sister were living, and they told them about the size of the yam Mass Mosquito was boasting about; and the Elephants trumpeted with laughter; and the seventeen of them ran to the tree in the jungle where ten parrots were living, and they told them about the enormous yam Mass Mosquito's father had reaped; then they ran and flew and wiggled around and told this story to everybody; and then all of them ran, flew and wiggled to Mass Mosquito's yard, and nearly killed him with questions.

Everybody was just laughing, and Brer Mosquito was getting more and more nervous, and they didn't let him tell the whole story, because each and everybody shouted and yelled and cried and roared: "A yam as big as yuh nose?"

"Yes, like mi nose," Mass Mosquito stammered. And the questions kept coming faster and faster, and faster and faster. Mass Mosquito had to answer: "Like mi nose...ke mi nose... mi nose... noooosssse... mi noossssse ossssse osssssssse ssssssssssssssss!"

And he jumped up, and he spread his wings, and he nodded, and he only was able to answer all questions with a "Sssssssssse!"

And from that day mosquitoes can not talk anymore. They only can whizz and buzz: "Sssssssssssssssssss..."

And whenever you are all alone in the bush or in a swamp or in your dark bedroom, and you hear this "Ssssssssss..." you know: this must be a mosquito.

Anancy mek it.

Jack Mandora, I just had to tell this story, especially because just now a mosquita – only female mosquitoes can bite! – has bitten me, and I have to rub vinegar on the spot to sooth the itching.

6

Anancy and the Birds

The most beautiful place on earth, Anancy said to himself and his friends, is my hammock which I have spread between two breadfruit-trees, with a cushion under my head. It swings easily, and after a short doze I open my eyes to watch the clouds sailing in the sky... And then I imagine faces in the clouds or animals or landscapes, and I close my eyes again and enjoy the pleasant breeze from the Tradewinds and...

"Yes, but if there was not this damned hunger!"

"Sometimes I feel like ah dead fi hungry! And how hard it is to be forced to get up and to find some food!"

Today, whole a flock of birds was sitting in the tree-top. It was a flock of Kling-Kling Birds, which was making a terrible noise – these birds were always hungry like Anancy –, and below the Kling-Kling-Birds, some parakeets were sitting on a limb, and they, too, made noise. Only way up, there in the sky, skillfully using the warm rising air, some John Crows were circling.

Anancy closed his eyes again. But his hungry belly did not let him fall asleep. Anancy sighed. This day is just too beautiful to waste it with... work.

He listened to the birds. And suddenly he heard a magic word, and he was wide awake!

"The dokanus are ripe now," a little Banana Quit chirped.

"In the hills North from here I saw a huge tree full of dokanus. It is time to reap them before the little boys from the village start flinging stones to get them down..."

Anancy licked his lips. First, he wondered why a Banana Quit spoke Standard English. Then, he thought of the hard work to make dokanus. Woiiii, this terrible work to crush the corn with mortar and pestle, to mix the flour with water, butter, nutmeg, cinnamon, sugar, and vanilla to get a thick dough, to turn it into balls, to wrap them up in a piece of banana-leaf as big as a rag, to put the pot on the fire...

No, as beautiful and delicious and heavenly the dokanus were tasting, Anancy was not in the mood to prepare them. That was simply too much hard work. Besides: Where could he get all these ingredients? Anancy had no money. And he could not get any credit.

Hm.

Yes, the birds lead a far easier life. They live like in paradise. They don't sow, they don't plant, they don't weed, they don't water the suckers, they don't spray the crop. They just fly around over pastures and bushland, and they sing... And the dokanus grow on trees – for them! What kind of injustice, Anancy thought. But then he remembered a bedtime-story his Granny used to tell him when he was small. It was about a man and his son who lived long, long time ago. Because of a wicked king they had to leave their country in a hurry. And so the father took some bird-feathers and bee's wax, and he made two pairs of wings, one for himself and one for his son. And father and son practised, and finally...they could fly! Yes, they could fly! But the father had warned his son not to fly too high. And the son – like lots of little boys – did not listen, and he flew higher and higher and higher, and nearer to the sun. And the wax melted, and the son dropped like a stone down to earth and was dead. Hm.

"If me dida him, me houlda fly just above de treetop-dem," Anancy said to himself. He then got an idea! He jumped up, took off his hat, bowed, and called with his sweetest voice: "Hallo, good mawning, Breddren and Sistren!"

All the birds became quiet immediately. They didn't trust human beings. Too often they had experienced how barefooted boys from the country got nearer, hiding a sling-shot behind their backs, and whistling peacefully. But then! These boys are out of order! They shot and killed and ate even little birds, not only pigeons and partridges.

But down there, this small guy with his funny hat, did not look like those small country-bumpkins with their running noses. And they could see clearly that he did not hide any sling-shot behind his back or in his pockets. This one must belong to that species that helps birds to survive in wintertime by spreading corn and hemp-seeds on the ground to feed them.

"Hm," the little Banana-Quit said, "can we help you?"

"Oh yes," Anancy laughed, "oonoo got so much nice feadders, and me did see how oonoo use fi mek a nes' wid de ole feadder-dem wha did fall out. Now, if each 'n' ebbryone ah oonoo woulda pull out one feadder each an gimmi, me woulda glue dem pon mi shoulder-dem an learn fi fly."

All the birds now laughed so loud that this attracted a chicken-hawk nearby, and he circled over the tree and got nearer and nearer. The birds were frightened. They were absolutely quiet.

"'xcuse," Anancy whispered, he bent down, grabbed a rock-stone, closed one eye, aimed well – and threw the stone, and hit the chicken-hawk hurting him. Six or seven feathers dropped to the ground, then the bird of prey disappeared.

"Dat was a good beginning ah fi we friendship, don't it?" Anancy cried. "Seen, me juss did help oonoo, and now me aks oonoo a small favour. Please, everybody juss gimme one, ongly one feadda, and den oonoo show me how fi fly."

The parakeets were especially grateful. Together with the parrots they were the biggest cowards, and when they became frightened, it could happen so that they dropped dead from a heart attack. So they started pulling out one feather each, and they helped Anancy to glue them with resin on to his shoulders.

Anancy now climbed on a tree, walked down a big limb, spread his wings, jumped and – landed on his belly. In vain the birds tried to suppress their laughter. But as they saw that Anancy did not give up, they respected him, and gave him some good advice. To drop down, to get up, to climb up the tree, to walk down a limb, to flutter with his wings, to jump – that is one thing. But after ten or eleven trials Anancy was able to fly some yards and to avoid a hard fall by putting up his wings.

"Respect! Respect!" the Kling-Kling Birds sang.

After one hour – Anancy was sweating hard – he flew with the flock of parakeets to the dokanu-tree.

But now the birds would experience Anancy's real character.

They could not know his greediness. There were enough dokanus for a family of twenty-five, but whenever a bird settled down on a bough, Anancy pushed him out of the way and shouted: "Ah me see it firs'!"

He stuffed the dokanus into his mouth, did not even chew, but swallowed like a puss, chased the next little bird and ate and ate and ate... It was outrageous!

Anancy now felt superior to birds. His heart rang joyfully: "I'm almighty now!"

Just gobbling and swallowing and pushing the birds out of his way, he thought about a future without hunger and hard work. He thought of the Pancake Trees he had heard about, of the Lolly-Trees, the Chewing Gum Trees and of the Candy Trees. He thought of all the avocado pears he could pick out of the tree-tops, of the sour-sops, the sweet-sops, the june-plums and the mangoes, the apples, and the guavas. Up to now he had to throw dozens of stones to get just a single fruit. Those days were now over!

A person who could fly, would finally be free of all worries about food. Not to mention that he was now able to tease the biggest and most dangerous animals like lions, tigers, elephants, crocodiles, buffaloes and snakes. He could flutter in front of their dangerous mouths full of sharp teeth just to fly up and doodoo on their heads... Yes, if he could steal a shotgun or a sling-shot he would turn into the Emperor of the Airforce: Hawks, eagles, falcons and vultures would have to pay tributes. In one word: Anancy had turned into a Superman now!

So he thought.

He did not watch all the birds around him which fluttered from one limb to the next and chatted to each other. And then all of them attacked Anancy! And they tore out the feathers they had donated. Anancy even lost the hawk's feathers, and in the confusion of wings and beaks Anancy

got dizzy, and he dropped to the ground. Bapps!

When Anancy woke up he was all alone. He rubbed his head, he tried to get up... His head, limbs and bones were hurting him, and when Anancy looked up to the tree-top he saw that the birds had finished all the dokanus. Not a single one was left for him. He had been greedy; and thus this fall was worse than that of the son in the story his granny had told him...

Instead of being the Emperor of the Air Force, instead of being a Superman, he was the little and weak Anancy again. He sighed. From that day people have tried to fly. The great painter, sculptor and engineer Leonardo da Vinci drew a flying-machine. But he could not fly with it. The famous taylor of Ulm, Germany, constructed a flying-machine, stood on the bridge crossing the Danube River, jumped and... fell into the water. It took mankind hundreds of years to invent the airplane.

Anancy mek it...

...that up to now no person can fly. And Anancy mek it that up to now even the smallest bird is laughing after us. And you and I who dream to be able to fly are still envious of the small bird called Hedge King who – a kind of Anancy himself – once flew higher than the proudest eagle.

Jack Mandora, me nuh chose none.

Anancy and Fire

Once upon a time Fire was a pretty, young woman living in the woodland. Her father was a lightning, her mother was a dead tree. She was very lonely as nobody talked to her, and nobody played with her. Most times she felt hungry. Only when the rainy season was over, she had enough food.

Sometimes Fire heard the birds in the trees talking about towns, villages, hamlets and houses inhabited by people. By all means she would have liked to see the inside of an house. But nobody invited her there.

One day Fire saw Anancy walking nearby through he woodland. She recognized him immediately: All the animals around used to talk about him. On the spot she fell in love with him. Thus she tried to draw his attention to herself. She danced around the stub of a tree she just had nibbled at; and she danced to the left, and gyrated to the right. (I'm sure you must have seen how a flame can dance). And Fire whistled, and she coo'd, and she hissed and snarled. Seeing this pretty little fire, Anancy stopped in his tracks and whistled and said: "Laaaaaawks, what a pretty gal!"

Fire bowed her head and blushed and asked coquettishly: "Yuh like me?"

Why, Anancy just loved how tenderly she asked him, and he thought: That must be love on first sight!

And he answered: "Gal, me like yuh like a bear likes honey, like ants like sugar; me like yuh like frog love water, me like yuh better dan candy an bake' sweet potatoes...!" Thus Fire started to dance a bit slower, bowed her head more, and blushed even more, and she asked him:" Ah true?"

"Yah, man," Anancy answered. "Me lov yuh so much

seh me wish we coulda live togedda. Ah whe yu ah live? Whe de house deh? Yuh ah live alone? Me woulda like fi move inna yuh yard right now!"

That was not exactly Fire's idea of love. She wanted to move out of the woodland and into her husband's yard with a pretty house with curtains at the windows and a wonderful thatch-roof. Thus she watched Anancy under her lowered lashes, and she said tenderly: "Sorry, me dear, nutten nuh go so. Me's still young, an' me live wid me madda. If she find out seh me ah chat wid a stranja, she woulda beat me, and put me under house-arrest..."

"Juss run 'way an live wid me!" Anancy cried.

"Me cyaan do dat," small, pretty Fire replied, and she swayed her hips.

"Come on," Anancy said, "if yuh lov me yuh juss run 'way an' live wid me, an' yuh manage fi me house, an' we live happily ever after wid lots ah pickney-dem. Juss come to me!"

"When?" Fire asked.

"Well, tonite. Ah wha yuh ah t'ink?"

"Yes, yes, yes," Fire cried, and she swayed her hips even more, wrang her hands, and smiled. "But whish place me can fine yuh? An' den..., Anancy, me likkle feet dem so tender, me cyaan walk barefoot so. If yuh really wan' seh me ah come to yuh, yuh haffi spread dry leaf-dem, boughs an branches, dry grass an coconut-tree fronds 'pon de grong fram right yah so to yuh house. An afta sun-down me gwaan run to yuh, an me stay wid yuh faevva."

"Ah nuh nuttin' dat, me lovely Fia," Anancy replied. "Me wish me coulda spread nuff roseblossom or dry-up nite-jasemin unda fi yuh pretty foot-dem. Me do as yuh seh. An nuh mek me wait 'pon yuh, come eight o'clock sharp!"

"Yes, me dear," Fire answered, and she blew him a kiss.

Why, fi me frien' dem shoulda see wha kinda pretty 'oman me got!, Anancy thought and he bowed and bided his farewell. He then turned around getting his machete out of its sheath, and he slashed dry limbs and grass, and he spread dry twigs, grass, flowers and blossoms on the way to his humble shack. And the most beautiful blossoms and flowers he spread from the threshold of the little house to the kitchen, to his living- and his bedroom. Having prepared everything for Fire's arrival he cooked some curry goat, his favourite food of which he thought that it would meet her taste. (Alàs, he could not know what a fire liked to eat...)

After that Anancy sat down in his favourite armchair on the verandah to wait for his future wife.

Anancy was so nervous that he puffed one pipe after the other, and he racked his brain how to name all the children he would have with Fire.

"Yes," he thought, "de firs' boy gwaan get a name startin' wid A. A like Anancy. De secon' pickny gwaan get a name dat start wid... B, de t'ird one wid C and so on, and so on."

But some letters gave him lots of problems. (Do you know first names which start with Q or X or Y or Z?)

Thus the time ran off so fast, that before Anancy could think of it, it was already eight 'o clock in the night.

Anancy looked up. But what is this? The whole forest near to his house seemed to be burning! A huge wall of fire was getting near to him. But what was getting nearer and nearer now was not the small, slim, elegant Miss Fire he'd met in the woodland, no, what was getting nearer and nearer and setting everything on fire and roared and threw

41

brimstone, was a huge, a fat, a superfat, a mampy Mrs. Fire!

Anancy was frightened, and he jumped up, and called: "Likkle Fire, dear Fire, sweet Miss Fire, go back! Me ah come tamarraw mawnin to yuh. Get back, me aks yuh! Go back whe yuh come fram! Ah wha de nex door-neighbours dem gwan seh when dem see yuh? T'ink of yuh madda! She gwaan beat yuh black an' blue! Is joke, a joke me ah mek. It ah outa orda if yuh move in yah so before we did marry."

But the huge Fire just watched him with bloodshot eyes, and opened her mouth as big as a barn-door, and she hissed and snarled, and she spat more fire, and whatever she touched went up in flames. This big wall of fire thundered towards Anancy's little house, and Anancy witnessed how it went up in flames and smoke, and although he repeatedly called for help... nobody heard him.

And from that day fires take pleasure in burning down barns, shacks, houses, hamlets, villages, even towns and cities.

Anancy mek it.

Jack Mandora, me nuh choose none. And from talking so much about fire I got thirsty, and I had to drink a shot of Jamaican rum which is so strong that it burns my throat. That is the reason why we call it "fire-water".

Anancy and Mongoose

Once upon a time unemployment hurt the people of the country terribly. And a long draught made farmers poorer and poorer. Whenever a worker or a farmer resorted to selling peanuts or cigarettes or matches or coconut-water, *The Royal Information Bulletin* proudly reported this as a success of the economy: "Self-Employment rose by 250%!"

Anancy and his mother were hurting bad. They did not have any work, did not have any cows, pigs or goats they could sell, they did not own a farm. They were very hungry.

One morning, Anancy's good friend, Brer Mongoose came running to Anancy's yard and yelled: "Hurry up, Anancy, hurry up! Me got information seh one farmer inna de nex' distric' will give a day's work for two smaddies. Hurry up befo' smaddy else hear 'bout i' an tell fi him frien'. Yuh can imagine how much smaddies gwaan stand inna line..."

So the two friends ran more than five miles to the next village. And when they knocked on the farmer's door, he said that they could start with the work right away: "De pay gonna be awright!"

If there is one thing Anancy used to hate then, was...hard

work. But he had no choice. Anancy's belly was rumbling, and one could see his ribs.

The whole day Anancy and Mongoose weeded and bushed a big piece of land. It was a very hot day. Anancy and Mongoose were covered with sweat. But at sunset the two of them had done a wonderful job. The farmer inspected his land and was full of praise for them.

"As you'll know," he said, "deh's lots ah farmer-dem wha tek advantage ah de unemployment and use fi abuse de working people bad. Dem pay dem cents and not dollars. But me respec' any hardworking' smaddy, an' it nuh matter wha kinda work him do. An' causen de two ah oonoo did wo'k hard an' reliable, an 'causen a holiday tomorrow, me gwaan gi' oonoo the agreed pay an' good-good bonus!"

Full of joy Mongoose jumped up, and Anancy threw his cap into the air. The farmer gave them their money, and led them to his barn where he used to store corn. He opened the door and waved his hand for them to follow him. The barn had only one window nearly under the roof. On the floor of the barn Anancy and his friend could see two ropes lying. They lead through this window to the back of the barn. One rope was very thin and fine, the other one was heavy and thick.

"Genklemen," said the farmer, "me tie de present-dem to dese ropes. Pick your choice!"

Anancy – as always – understood faster, and thus he jumped to the big rope, and grabbed it. So Brer Mongoose had to take the thin rope.

But imagine their surprise when the two of them, ropes in their hands, climbed upon a table under the window, and peeped into the backyard: The farmer had tied the thin rope to a fat ox, and a chicken was tied to the thick rope...

45

Anancy was vexed, he was vexed indeed, he was vexed with himself. He nearly fainted. But then he put a good face upon it, he expressed his thanks to the farmer, and left the barn. His friend stammered his thanks to the generous employer, and followed his friend. In the backyard they grabbed for their ropes, and they started to lead their animals to their respective yards. But as soon they had left the farmer's yard, Anancy smiled and said: "Listen now, me frien', it ah get dark awready, and me nuh want seh suppen bad gwaan happen to yuh an yuh ox. Jus spen' de night inna fi me yard. An' tomorrow mawnin' yuh can reach yuh yard safe-safe."

"T'anks very much," Brer Mongoose agreed, and he followed Anancy.

After having reached Anancy's yard, they shared a meal of roasted yams. Then they wiped off with water from a drum standing under the gutter of the roof, and they felt tired enough to have a good night's sleep. Brer Mangoose was getting Anancy's small bedroom, while the host put up with a narrow bed in the kitchen.

Anancy lay down on it, and shut his eyes. But he did not sleep. He was listening to Brer Mongoose's snoring... And then he got up, and he tiptoed into the yard. In the dark of the night Anancy tied a thick cloth around the snout of the ox, he took the machete out of its sheeth, and with one big stroke he chopped off the ox's tail!

Then he dug a hole into the ground, put half of the tail into it, and covered the hole with dirt and sand. Having done this, he led the ox to a small piece of woodland, and tied it to a tree. The poor ox could not even moo because its snout was muzzled.

Anancy tiptoed back to the house and to his kitchen,

and went to sleep.

The next morning, Anancy boiled a big bowl of turned corn-meal for breakfast. After that he entered his bedroom to wake Brer Mongoose who was very grateful.

"Yuh really is a good-good frien', Anancy," he stammered. They ate their breakfast, and while Brer Mongoose washed the dishes, Anancy stood at the door of his house, he yawned, he stretched, and peeped into his yard.

"But what is this," Anancy exclaimed. "Come, Brer Mongoose, come fas'-fas'! Woiiiii! Now me know why me did wake up inna de miggle ah de night. Me did feel an eart'quake. An eart'quake, Brer Mongoose! An' imagine: Fi yuh ox gone! Him disappear inna de ground! Me ongly see him tail wha stick outa de groun'!"

Fast like lightning Brer Mongoose ran into the yard, and pulled the ox' tail with all his force – and then he dropped backward with the tail in his hands. Anancy started to cry,

and he sobbed: "Poor breddren! Poor Brer Mongoose! Yuh did wo'k so hard, an' yuh really deserve de ox. An' now, wha' happen? Yuh ox lass, yuh lass de ox!" Brer Mongoose, started to cry with disappointment. And he cried, and he cursed, and he swore that never ever again he'd eat ox-tail, that he never ever again would enjoy eating beef.

Anancy pretended to feel sorry for him, and said: "Me cyaan stan' fi see adda people suffer. Yuh know suppen, Brer Mongoose, yuh tek fi me chicken, an' me tek fi yuh ox-tail."

Now Brer Mongoose stopped crying, and smiled, deeply moved. He told Anancy: "T'anks, Anancy! Ah dat me call frien'ship. Yuh's a really a fine breddren! Bot me cyaan accep yuh offer..."

But Anancy was successful in convincing him in the long run, and in the end Brer Mangoose left the yard with Anancy's chicken.

From that day, mongooses like chicken-meat. From that day they just sneak into chicken-coops to kill and eat chicken and roosters.

Anancy mek it.

9

Anancy and Wasp

*L*ong, long time ago Brer Wasp was a Don, the god-father of his neighbourhood, He was an elegant guy, always "dressed up to the max" boasting two big revolvers, and whenever he opened his mouth to curse or to give orders, people could see two rows of white, shining teeth. Yes, in those days wasps had teeth.

Well, Brer Wasp was very proud of his teeth, and he used to brush them three times a day. Even when it seemed fit to be serious, Brer Wasp used to smile and laugh to show off with his wonderful clean and white teeth. Sometimes he used to grind them to show off, sometimes when everybody was watching him he used to bite into apples and carrots, yes, he even bit off pieces of cola-nuts, and always be used to crack chicken-bones, beef-bones, pork-bones and goat-bones just to show how strong his teeth were. And quite often he used to bite...people and animals. Sometimes he injured them badly just to show how sharp his teeth were. That was the reason why nearly all the people around could not stand him.

Well, Brer Anancy did not like Wasp at all. And he was furious with him because Wasp was always idle. Wasp had inherited a big house and lots of money, and if he needed more money he promised to protect people who did not

need any protection. But they would have to pay Wasp for this... protection. Anancy earned his living as a pushcart-man. Times were hard, very hard.

Well, one day when Anancy pushed his cart to a hill-top, sweating and out of breath, he bumped into Brer Wasp who was surrounded by a big crowd. Wasp showed his tricks with the revolver, and he boasted badly, and as always he showed his big, white teeth. Anancy watched him silently, wiped the sweat from his forehead, and then it was that he decided to teach Wasp a lesson.

So he put on his best smile, and he got near to Brer Wasp and shouted: "Hi, Brer Wasp! How t'ings?"

"Good-good," Wasp laughed, "as always. An' yuh? Yuh awright?"

"Awright?" Anancy cried. "Not at all-tall! De wo'k too hard, man. Me's a likkle, weak man, an' fi push dis yah cart it ah mash' me up." And full of admiration, he watched Brer Wasp from near: "Yes, man, if me did 'trong like yuh, de wo'k houlda easier. If me did trong like yuh me houlda jus' laugh 'bout hard work. Me wish yuh coulda be me for a while, and me could live a good life like yuh. Me woulda do ebbryting fi dat!"

"Ebbryt'ing, Brer Nancy?" Wasp laughed. "Ah true?"

"Yeah, man!"

"Supposen," Wasp continued slyly, "me do yuh wo'k fi a week or two, ah wha' you gwaan gimme?"

Anancy did not need time to find an answer: "Well, sah," he replied, "if yuh do fi mi pushcart-wo'k fa two weeks me houlda give yuh a good-good bite outa me flesh. Yuh may bite anyt'ing – but not fi me head. Me head too tuff fi yuh teet' dem."

Brer Wasp was getting furious now: "Too tuff, man? Nuttin too tuff fi me teet'!"

"Ah true?" Anancy pretended to admire Wasp.

"True-true," Wasp replied. "Fi yuh head a small matta fi me teet'!"

For the next two weeks the neighbourhood saw Brer Wasp pushing Anancy's push-cart with ease. Wealthy ladies asked market-woman to load up the cart so that Brer Wasp could push the heavy load to their houses. Farmers shopping in hardware-stores would load the cart with blocks, lumber and zinc-sheets so that Brer Wasp had to push it with all his force. But always he was smiling, and he showed his big, white, beautiful teeth.

In the meantime, Anancy enjoyed his holidays. He lay in his hammock between two breadfruit-trees, read books, and smoked his pipe. One morning he walked towards the Parish Council's garbage-dump, and picked up a big, blackened dutch-pot with two small holes in the bottom. Then he went to a welder and begged him to cut two small holes into the side of the pot with his torch. The welder laughed and did Anancy this favour.

After two weeks, on a Saturday morning, Brer Wasp approached Anancy's yard. He was very eager to teach Anancy a lesson and to bite a piece... out of Anancy's head! He knocked on Anancy's door. No answer. He knocked again, this time very hard. Bang, bang, bang!

Anancy was lying on his bed in the bedroom. The bedroom was very dark. Anancy had closed the shutters tight, so that the room was in nearly complete darkness, and nobody could see that he had covered his face with the dutch-pot. Only the white in his eyes could be seen through the holes in the pot. Brer Wasp was knocking louder and louder. Finally he heard Anancy's feeble voice: "Come in, Brer Wasp! Me nuh feel good at all. Me is sick bad."

Wasp entered the bedroom. After a while his eyes could make out a shadow on the bed.

"Anancy!" Brer Wasp roared now. "Me ready fe a good-good bite! It nuh matter seh yuh's sick. Yuh did promise if me do yuh wo'k fi two weeks, me coulda tek me bite outa yuh flesh. An' me come fi tek a good bite outa yuh head as promised. Yuh 'member?"

"Me use fi keep me promise, Brer Wasp," Anancy whispered. "Me's a man ah honour. Come, tek wha yuh wan' fi tek!"

Now Brer Wasp opened his mouth very, very wide, and he took... a good bite! Errrrrks! Krrrrrrks! And all his good teeth broke up and fell on the floor! (Because he did not bite into Anancy's flesh but into the dutch-pot. Do you remember that?)

From this day wasps don't have anymore teeth!
Anancy mek it.

After a while wasps got small stings. They no longer
boast with guns anymore. They became shy. You can now
see them flying around with their brothers and sisters. They
like sugar, sweets and porridge. And with their small stings
they do not attack you deliberately. They only do it in self-
defence. If you harm them they'll defend themselves.
Whenever you don't do any harm to them they leave you
alone. They have learned their lesson.

Yes, all this and more,

Anancy mek it.

10

Anancy and Crocodile

*T*he hot summer months were over, and it was getting cooler. Anancy was pleased as now the breadfruit-trees were bearing. He just had to pick the breadfruits; and with the showers in the nights the rivers were full of water again, and Anancy could do what he liked to do most – catch crayfish. In the mango-season he did not bother to cook; he just turned the pot down and ate only mangoes, morning, noon and night. And in the bread-fruit-seasons he stuck to breadfruit. Boiled breadfruit, bread-fruit-fritters, breadfruit-balls, roast breadfruit, breadfruit stewed in coconut milk (run-down)... Yeah, man! And then crayfish! Anancy loved crayfish-soup and curry-crayfish but liked best, crayfish steamed with onions, garlic, tomatoes, bell-peppers, skellion and thyme...

Not far from the river-mouth a kind of barricade made up of sand and gravel had been created, and therefore further up the river-course the fast-running water expanded and encircled a small island. There Anancy was squatting on boulders, and cautiously he turned every stone and small boulder. Aha! How the crayfish escaped to try hiding under the stones! Aha! And how Anancy grabbed them and threw them into a bucket! He hardly could wait to drop them into the pot...

Now the first bucket was full, the second-one half-full. It started to drizzle. It did not matter to Anancy. In his hunting fever he forgot that at the upper course of the river it must have rained heavily already. He did not pay attention to the clouds gathering at the mountain-top. He was just glad that the sun did not burn anymore... Thus the current was getting faster, and the two river-arms enclosing the small island were getting deeper and deeper. Far too late Anancy noticed that the water had become too deep to wade through to the banking. The water gurgled alongside him, it carried dead goats and uprooted trees along. Now Anancy was getting terribly frightened!

He hoped that the swelling river would burst the barrier between the pond and the sea the rivermouth had formed so that after a good while the water level would have fallen so much, that Anancy very carefully could wade through the riverbed to reach the banking...

The shower stopped as fast as it had began. But now it was getting dark! Anancy was getting frightened again. And he was right, because now as he looked down the rivercourse, he saw some tree-trunks, very long tree-trunks which lay beside the river...gliding into the water. And swam towards him – against the current!

Anancy suppressed a shout. He placed his hand on his lips. Because: These were not tree-trunks! These were the big crocodiles – more than twelve feet long! – who lived not far from the rivermouth. Suppose they saw him, too... Totally shocked, Anancy looked out for help. But here no shotguns were growing in trees. Here not even a guango-tree could be seen, not a fig-tree, neither a duppy-tree full of wist he could use to climb...

He imagined the ugly reptiles' sharp teeth aimed at him.

Teeth which could bite a wild boar in two with one snap!
Anancy closed his eyes, and he racked his brain to find
an escape, a chance to escape a terrible death by being
bitten by a crocodile. Anancy imagined how one of these
monsters would tear him apart while the other crocodiles
were getting nearer to get their share... He nearly fainted!

But then he got an idea. He opened his eyes. It looked
as if the crocodiles had not seen him yet. And so he said
to himself: Attack is the best defence, and so he jumped
up, and began to dance on the spot, waving his arms,
throwing his hat into the air, and shouting "Yow! Come
rite yah so, Brer Crocodile!"

And the huge reptile which was nearest to him, opened
his huge snout, blinked his eyes in surprise, and stammered:
"Me's nobody's brother, man, me's Olga..."

"Oh, Sis Olga," Anansi cried, "most beautiful of all she-
crocodile widin ten miles, mek me hug yuh up, cousin Olga!"

"Yuh cousin?" The reptile replied. "Me nuh know nuttin'
'bout any likkle, ugly cousin like yuh." And it waddled
ashore.

"But what is this?" Anancy shouted. "Fi yuh Mumma
nevva tell yuh bout me? She did hole me ova de baptismal
font. She's fi me Godmadda! Yeah, man, me's yuh cousin,
an' as a present me carry whole ah bucket ah crayfish fi
yuh."

He told the crocodile why and how he got stuck on this
tiny island in the middle of the river, and he asked the
crocodile-lady to carry him through the river to the banking.

"Dat unbelievable," Olga whispered, and then she roared,
"If yuh wasn't fi me cousin, me woulda nyam yuh rite yah
so!"

"Me know," Anancy replied, "yuh's famous fi dat.

Come, me invite yuh fi dinner. Mek we run-dong de crayfish, mek me simmer dem inna coconut-milk!"

"Noah," Crocodile Olga grunted, "me ongly nyam raw meat."

"Raw meat?" Anancy cried.

"Yes, man, me juss bite-up ebbryt'ing delicious, an' swallow it. An' rite now, me got suppen better fi do dan cook fi yuh..."

"Whateva it may be, me gwaan help yuh, dear cousin," Anancy said, and he jumped on the crocodile's back. He did not look to the right, neither to the left. He was afraid

of all these other crocodiles' looks. Crocodile-lady Olga glided into the water and swam where she had come from. Without making any noise the other monsters followed her. Anancy felt their hungry eyes on his little backside, the only piece of flesh on him that might be worthy of a good bite.

As soon as the crocodiles reached the river-bank, Anancy turned around, and to his great surprise he noticed how all these dangerous reptiles cast warm and tender glances and they bid him a tender farewell, and all of them waddled to different spots along the river. Surprised he turned to the crocodile he had called cousin to save his life, and he noticed the same tender expression on Olga's face.

"Come," she warmly said, "it ah time fi wash de egg-dem."

"Me can do dat fi yuh," Anancy replied, "In de meantime, yuh can cook fi me..."

"Me nuh cook," Olga roared. "Lissen good-good! Me tek de egg dem outa de basket, an yuh polish dem – seen, how me truss yuh? – an yuh gi' dem back to me."

"No, no," Anancy said, "betta de odder way roun'. Yuh's de madda, an' as all good maddas yuh know how fi dress-up, dress-up an' sweet up de pickney-dem fi Sunday. Juss' imagine seh me drop an egg by mistake. Dat houlda terrible!"

So crocodile Olga waddled to her house, and after a short while she came back with a basket and a leather-rug.

They walked to the river. Up the rivercourse, half a dozen female crocodiles could be seen taking eggs out of baskets, washing them, drying them, and putting them back.

Olga handed Anancy her basket, he placed it on the earth, took an egg out of the basket, handed it to Olga – to his astonishment, it was clean already –, and he counted: "One."

Without turning around Olga repeated: "One," breathed on the egg, cleaned it tenderly, held it against the light, and gave it back to Anancy. He took out the second egg, sucked it out, and – he handed back the first, clean egg to Olga.

"Two," Anancy said.

"Yes, two," Olga agreed. Anancy sucked the next egg out of the basket. Without turning her head Olga gave him back the cleaned egg.

"Three," Anancy shouted, and he sucked out the next egg. Each time he handed over the very same, clean egg to Olga. Nine other eggs – he sucked out.

Then, he covered the nine sucked-out eggs and the one that was cleaned all the while with a kitchen-towel as he had seen it when Olga carried the basket. And so it was he who carried the basket to the hatching-hut.

Coming back he saw Olga flossing her dangerous lower jaw teeth smiling at him.

"Well, afta we done fi we work, yuh's suppose' fi help me reach de odder river-bank," Anancy cried hoping the reptile would not notice the trembling of his voice. He just grabbed the two buckets with the cray-fish, jumped on Olga's back, and pressed his heels into her sides. She waddled to the river-bank, and glided into the water.

"If yuh wasn't me cousin me houlda...," Olga roared and laughed.

"But cousin," Anancy smiled, "me's too mawga..."

"Mawga, me neckback," Olga cried, "me nevva mek a nice, likkle snack pass me..."

They reached the other bank, and when Anancy was about to bid a short, but polite farewell, they could hear a huge noise from the other river bank. Olga's best sistren had just discovered that in her basket nine of ten eggs were sucked out. Fast like lightning Anancy grabbed his buckets

and ran as fast as possible.

Too late crocodile Olga realized how Anancy had tricked her. It was the first time a huge monster like a croc bawled and shedded tears. From that day, we call this "crocodile-tears." And from that day all of us – man and woman, boy and girl, and all animals take good care not to get too near to crocodiles. For if you get too near to one it will remember how a tiny, facety man had tricked a crocodile. That is the reason why all crocodiles want to take revenge.

Anancy mek it.

Anancy and Pattoo

Once upon a time Owl was a happy man and always in a joking mood. He was a bus-driver and used to work from nine to five, five days a week, and made a decent living. He had lots of friends who called him Brer Pattoo, he was a member of a choral society, and was president of the Amateur Magicians' Association. Only one thing used to bother him deeply: The women and girls did not like him because of his greyish brown plumage and his big, green, protruding eyes.

Well, one day he met Anancy on the road, and he invited him to an ice-cream. Anancy could not say No. He just loved ice-cream. They entered an ice-cream-parlour which was run by an Italian. How, their mouths started to water when they saw Brer Francesco prepare a banana-split: He peeled six ripe chiney-bananas, halved them lengthwise, and placed them onto oval glass-platters. Between the halved bananas he placed some ice-cream balls on which he poured melba-sauce with peanuts. Onto the upper banana-halves he sprayed a large amount of whipped cream, and decorated whole the thing with some Merino-cherries.

Can you imagine how Brer Pattoo and Anancy relished these banana-splits? Well, they took their time to eat this treat. But after that, Anancy realised that his friend was

looking sad.

"Wha' happen to yuh, me frien'?" Anancy asked. "Yuh's looking too sad."

"Yes, Brer Anancy, one might say dat," Pattoo replied after a while. "Yuh's famous fi be a man who' can help himself. Nobody evva gwaan figat how yuh trick Sis Yellow Snake. An' yuh's de ongly one who forced de King ah de animal-dem, Brer Lion, fi keep him promise. Most ah de politician-dem nevva do dat..."

"Mek it short, Brer Pattoo," Annancy said and smiled. "Ah wha sadden yuh? Me bet seh dat mussi a ooman-problem!"

Brer Pattoo's eyes were getting bigger, and he cried: "How yuh know? Ah true, me hav bad luck wid de ooman-dem. Dem nuh like me. Dem seh me ugly. Untrut', dat!

Dem nuh like me feadda-dem. But adda birds hav feaddas, too, an dem hav girl-friends to fetch! An dem say dem nuh like me darkers. But, Anancy, me haffi wear darkers causen me eye-dem cyaan stan' de bright sunshine. Wha me's suppose' fi do?"

"No problem, Brer Pattoo," Anancy replied. "If yuh cyaan enter de house t'rough de front-door yuh tek de back-door. Yuh know suppen? Mek we go ah Ooman Town. Ah deh so dem hav pretty an' nice gals an' oomen. Inna de olden days, grandee Nanny, de Ashanti Princess did found dat town so dat de English soljamen couldn't fine dem. But firs', me len' yuh one ah me pretty-pretty shirt-dem, an' a jacket, an a name-bran' tie. An' den yuh gwaan see seh alla de pretty ooman-dem gwaan fall fi yuh!"

"Yuh really is a good-good frien', Anancy," Pattoo sighed. And they did what Anancy had proposed.

But whenever he made a proposal, Anancy had something different on his mind: Long time he had planned to go to Woman Town, but he was afraid of seeing the women there without a strong bodyguard. The women in Woman Town were proud and independent-minded, they wouldn't let a useless man rule them.

After having reached Woman Town, Anancy and his friend walked straight to the market-square. Anancy took a mouth-organ out of his pocket, and started to play a nice melody. Immediately all the women were gathering around him, young and old, pretty and less pretty, slim and fat. Because they knew:

> Whe dem ah play music
> yuh can sekkle dong;
> causen nasty people dem
> nuh sing no song.

Now Anancy gave the prettiest women a wink, and he started to sing:

See yah, Anancy ah come,
Him sing a song fi yuh alone;
All de gal-dem sing an' cry:
We love Anancy, eyeyey!

Nobody paid attention to Brer Pattoo. All the girls and women turned their back to him. All eyes were on Anancy. But wait, Brer Pattoo told himself, Anancy is a ginnal. But watch out, me learn me lesson.

Thus Brer Pattoo formed his beak like a trumpet, and he started to play a sweeter tune than Anancy's. Now all the woman and girls nudged each other, and they turned to Brer Pottoo. Nobody paid anymore attention to Anancy. Everybody danced around Brer Pattoo. And Brer Pattoo started to sing. And how he could sing! He got a wonderful baritone-voice:

In Ooman Town, in Ooman Town
De ooman-dem fed up wid boredom;
Dat's why me come yah an sing fi dem
De sweetes' an' wickedes' tune.

Me's not a Bredda Do-No-Good
Like dat smaddy
Me's a hard-working man
Wid an heart as good as gole...

But Anancy interrupted him: "Brer Pattoo, gimme back me shirt right now!" It looked as if Anancy was beside himself with rage.

"Hush, please, Brer Anancy!" Brer Pattoo begged.

"Nuh hush me to rahtid," Anancy cried. "Gimme back me shirt right now!"

"But Anancy," Pattoo stammered, "yuh promise..."

"Me nuh promise nuttin!" Anancy cried. "Gimme back fi me t'ings!"

And he ran to Brer Pattoo, and he tore off Brer Pattoos tie, shirt and jacket.

Brer Pattoo couldn't say a word! His voice failed. He only could sigh and moan and bawl: "Ooooohoooo!"

The women drew back from him. They trembled with disgust.

Only a few of them felt sorry for Brer Pattoo.

Thus Brer Pattoo left the market-square as fast as possible, and ran and ran, and left Woman Town behind; and from that day owls are hiding during the day, and leave their hiding-place only in the night, so that nobody can see them.

Anancy mek it.

Jack Mandora, me nuh choose none.

Anancy and How Crab Got His Shell

Once upon a time there was an old woman. Her name was Miss Brown. But as she was very rich and arrogant she did not like her name. Therefore she decided to call herself secretly, Miss Hoitytoity. Her husband had died some years ago, and Mrs. Brown had no children. So she decided to adopt some pets as children.

Soon Mrs. Brown had a puppy, three little kitten, lots of chickens, a parrot, two little ramgoats, five parakeets and a jaunty, little crab. She spoilt them with sweeties and biscuits, used to bathe them twice a day, sprayed cologne on their necks, and bought them useless toys with which the birds and small pets used to play for two or three days to leave them damaged in a corner. Maybe you know one of these old little ladies living uptown who treat their pets like children. They put small shoes on their dogs, decorate their kitten with pretty ribbons, and they give their animals better food than poor people can afford for themselves.

Yes, Mrs. Brown loved her pets. But she could not stand people. Her helpers were badly paid, Mrs. Brown gave them so-so dumplings and herb-tea for breakfast and a cheap porridge for lunch, she subtracted lots of money whenever a helper was five minutes late for work, and she wrote bad references whenever the helpers dared quit their jobs. But the worst thing was how she treated the girls and women who applied for a job as a washer-woman. In those days there was no piped water in the houses, and nobody had a washing-machine. Thus the woman had to carry the baskets with dirty laundry to the river. They had to stand in the cold water, to wash there, and they had to hit the heavy, water-soaked sheets on the boulders in the river before they put them onto the grass near the riverbank. Mrs. Brown promised the washer-women good food, free lodging and a very good pay if the women washed very well and... if they could guess Mrs. Brown's nickname. Well in those days like nowadays unemployment was hurting many, many people, and each and every week a new woman or a girl turned up to wash for Mrs. Brown hoping to be able to guess her nickname.

But whatever they guessed, they could not find out the name their employer had given herself. Lots of them would cry after having failed; and Mrs. Brown pretended to feel sorry for them, and she took out a calabash to catch their tears with it – and used to give only some water-biscuits to those poor things. Nothing else. You can imagine how fast the calabash was full of tears... And the people started to guess what the old lady intended to do with these tears. Many people said that Mrs. Brown was a witch or an obeah-

dared speak out.

Well, Anancy heard about these rumours. He was unemployed, too. Though he was not a girl or woman, he could wash, clean, wipe and dust, he could babysit and cook. All these things his granny had taught him when she raised him.

Anancy did not like what he heard about Mrs. Brown. Not at all. And so he decided to put an end to her wicked ways. He lay down in his hammock, smoked his pipe, and racked his brain. Finally he got it: The weak point of this clever, mean and nasty old woman must be... her adopted children, must be her pets. Hm...

So Anancy disguised himself as a young woman and walked to Mrs. Brown's villa. She showed him the laundry-basket, and she gave him soap and brush. Anancy carried the basket on his head to the river which was far away.

The sun was hot. Anancy scrubbed the dirty clothes and sheets, he was sweating hard. After a while, he saw a little crab waddling by. (In those days crabs had no shells. The skin on the back of a crab was smooth, warm, and silky like that of a snake.)

Anancy whistled after crab. The little crab never lived to see the day that a girl would whistle after him. He started to get proud, he lifted his head, and tried to waddle more elegantly.

Anancy bowed his head and whispered – but in a way crab could hear him: "Woiiiii, what a handsome guy!"

The little crab blushed and stopped in his tracks.

"Yuh like me-me-me?" he stammered.

"Yessah!" Anancy cried. "Me love yuh like frog love water. My, juss seeing how elegant yuh set yuh foot when yuh ah walk, it ah break me heart! Yuh got style an' manners. Yuh mussi study ah foreign, Sir."

Never before a man or animal had flattered crab so. So he played humble and said: "My, one comes around, me dear. An' me can tell yuh seh nowhe' me did see such a nice an' clever gal like yuh. Me really like yuh, an whenevva me can do suppen fi yuh, juss tell me, yuh hear?"

Anancy held his breath and blushed, "You flatter me, Sir. But me's not from yah so, an' me nuh t'ink we'll see each adda again. But me always will 'memba yuh, promise."

So the little crab eagerly answered: "Soon be back, Beautiful!" And he waddled away.

Got him, Anancy told himself, and when he saw theat crab was coming back after a short while, he spat into his palm and rubbed the spit under his eyes so that it looked like tears.

"Woooiiii, woii, poor me!" Anancy sobbed. "Lawdamassi, ah wha me a go do?"

"W'happen to yuh, me Beautiful?" the little crab asked.

Anancy sobbed. "Yuh know whole day me ah wo'k for old Mrs. Brown. An' now she a tell me seh if me nuh fine out har nickname me nuh get a single cent. Poor girl-child, me! How me can buy medicine fi me ole an' sick madda?"

"Please, please, nuh bawl," Crab begged him. "De ole lady ah fi me madda, an' me know har name."

"Oh please, tell me now," Anancy cried. "Tell me now! Me nuh know wha fi do. An yuh did promise fi help me when me need help."

"If yuh help me, Sah, me go ah movie-theatre wid yuh nex' Sunday, even if me haffi walk five miles fi reach deh. Woiii, me really did fall in love wid yuh!"

"Dat awrite, gal," Crab said. "Me keep me promise. De name ah me old lady is... Madda Hoitytoity."

And sadly he added: "But me cyaan go to a movie wid yuh. Me's not allowed fi go ah road afta six."

Anancy kissed Crab on his cheek, and went on washing. In the late afternoon, he folded the dry laundry, put it into the basket, heaved it unto his head, and ran to Mrs. Brown's yard.

Mrs. Brown inspected each and every piece of the washed clothes and sheets, nodding satisfied, then she sat down in her armchair on the verandah, and asked affably: "Well, gal, yuh know fi me nickname?"

"Me nuh sure, Ma'm," Anancy stammered.

"Yuh got t'ree chance fi guess de name, gal," the old lady said and grinned scornfully.

"Fi yuh name is... Madda Clebba?"

"No!"

"Fi yuh name is... Madda Mawga?"

"No , gal!"

"Or is yuh name... is yuh name.. Yuh name Madda Hoitytoity?"

The old Mrs. Brown nearly fainted when she heard the right answer. But then she got up, walked into the kitchen, loaded a big box with first-class foodstuff, gave it to Anancy, and removed a pack of money hidden between her breasts, out of which she took a good amount, and handed it to her... "o.k., Anancy."

Anancy then told Mrs. Brown that he would be unable to move into her house as a helper and washer because her mother was very sick, and he bowed deep, and...disappeared.

The mean Mrs. Brown a.ka. Hoitytoity slowly sat down in her armchair, closed her eyes, and racked her brain: Who could have blown her secret? Only her children. Yes, one of the children, one of her pets must have told it to the girl. Mrs. Brown jumped up and called the pets into her living-room.

"Ah which one ah oonoo ugly country-bumpkin did disclose me name?" She asked furiously.

"Me nuh ugly country-bumpkin," Crab murmured.

"Ah wha yuh ah whisper, son?" Mrs. Brown shouted. But she had heard what he said. "One more time: Ah which one ah oonoo tell dis-yah ugly an' dunce country-gal fi me name? Mussi yuh, likkle Parrot!"

"Ah nuh me!" Parrot shouted. And she whispered: "Why she always ah call me Pa-rrot? Me's a gal. An' so me name ah Ma-rrot."

"Ah wha yuh ah whisper, Son?" Mrs. Brown shouted.

"Nutten," Likkle Parrot or Marrot answered.

"She no ugly an' dunce country-gal," Little Crab whispered again.

"Ohhh, me likkle Crab, yuh did see him, don't it?"

Mrs. Brown 's eyes shone. "Den it was yuh wha tell de gal me name, don't it?"

Mrs. Brown's voice sounded sweet. But all the pets knew too well what this meant. They tried to look as small as possible. They were terribly afraid of Mrs. Brown whenever her voice was sweet like sugar.

"Me's not a traitor." Crab cried hopelessly. "Me juss like justice fi rule. All ah de woman-dem, an' de girl-dem wha use fi come right yah so fi get a job as a washer-ooman... Yuh cheat all ah dem! Yes, cheat dem, an' den yuh nevva pay dem!"

"But wait," Mrs. Brown shouted furiously. All her children, the pets wished they were invisible. Then the old woman ran to her chest-of-drawers, grabbed the calabash with both hands, she poured the tears in the calabash on Crab's back, and then she pressed the calabash with all her force on Little Crab's back. Where it got stuck. In vain the crab tried to get rid of it. He shook his shoulders, he dropped down, he rolled his back on the ground. But the

calabash was glued to his back.
From that day crabs have shells.

Anancy mek it.

Jack Mandora, me nuh choose none.

13

Anancy and the Power of Music

Once more the bailiff came and brought the eviction order, because, Anancy always resisted paying rent for the house he lived in.

"Shelter," Anancy used to cry, "should be free like the air we breathe!"

Thus Anancy was forced to squat a piece of land on a hill where other squatters had made up some shacks already. The land did not belong to them. The hill they were living on was "Crown Land." And the Crown was... Brer Lion! Every day he planned to get rid of the squatters by sending the police and a bulldozer. The Lion just did not care. He was very rich, and below the hill they could see the plains where sugar-cane and corn was planted. Even this domain was owned by the Crown which employed rangers in uniforms who guarded the land and the crop. Thus the poor people could not steal food.

In front of Anancy's shack lived Mr. Smith and his big family. Mr. Smith earned a living by felling trees in the woodland – which was owned by the Crown, too – and by burning char-coal he would sell. Like most poor people he liked pets. He had a whole pack of half-starved mongrels, which barked day and night and sometimes even bit little children who passed by on the little road. But if a burglar turned up in the night the dogs were of no use. On the zinc-roof of the charcoal-burner's little house, the pigeons coo'd.

Anancy shared his shack with Brer Turtle. Quite often with their eyes the two of them followed the pigeons who would fly to one of the corn-fields and help themselves to some juicy kernels of corn.

"Laaawks!" the turtle sighed. "One shoulda have wings, too!"

Anancy did not say a word. He had given up his dream of being able to fly. He lay down in his hammock, lighted his pipe, and he racked his brain...

Well, Brer Turtle wished to be able to fly. Supposed, he was able to help Brer Turtle to make his dreams come true...

The next morning, Anancy called the pigeons and told them about Brer Turtle's wish. The pigeons started laughing.

"'top dat!" Anancy cried, "Poor people's dreams are their Kingdom of Heaven. An it shoulda easy fi oonoo fi mek him dream come true. Oonoo juss haffi len' him some feaddas."

The pigeons agreed. But to be on the safe side they took advice from the oldest he-pigeon who as people said was as wise as an owl. To their surprise the old pigeon approved of Anancy's proposal. Thus each pigeon sacrificed some feathers and helped Anancy to glue them on Turtle's back. And now Brer Turtle started to practise. And how he practised! With all these feathers on his back he was looking like a pin-cushion, but whatever he tried he was unable to fly properly. His body was too heavy. But when he climbed on the roof-top and took a run and jumped, he was able to fly a little. Turtle practised each day, and every day he would fly a little bit further. On a beautiful Sunday, when nobody was working in the fields, Anancy and his friend climbed on the roof-top, and Anancy gave Brer Turtle good advice how to fly even further.

"An' when yuh lan', Breddren, yuh fi mek a slight right bend agains' de breeze. Den yuh nuh gwaan drop pon de ground too hard. Here, tek dat basket. Ova deh so, whe de ranger-dem cyaan see yuh, yuh collec' all de kernel ah corn wha lie deh pon de groun'. Causen if de corn plant-dem swing de rangerman-dem a go notice dat an' gwaan ketch yuh. When de basket full-up yuh haffi crawl carefully to dat deh corner deh. Ah deh so, me ah wait fi yuh. An den yuh gimmi de basket, an yuh can crawl unda de barb' wire. An lata, we gwaan mash de kernel dem wid morta an pestle, an we gwaan mek corn-meal, an outa de corn-meal we gwaan mek de nices' dishes. Don't it? But if dem ah catch yuh, please, nuh resis'! Juss follow back ah dem an... sing!"

"Sing?" Brer Turtle asked wonderingly.

"Yah, man, juss sing," Anancy repeated. "Yuh've got de mos' beautiful voice round yah so, a great tenor-voice, and wid dat yuh can soften-up ebbrybuddy's heart. Yuh nevva see how de she-pigeon an de cock-pigeon hug up an kiss up, whenevva dem ah hear yuh?"

"Yes, but de pigeon-dem dem hav' a heart but de ranger-man dem an de police-dem hav' no heart," his friend made him think.

"Juss put yuh trust inna de power of music!" Anancy cried. "When dem ah catch yuh, sing fa yuh life!"

I'm not a nightingale, Brer Turtle thought but he did not tell this to his friend. He put the basket on his back, climbed on the roof-top, took a good run and... jumped. The breeze

carried him to the corn-field. Brer Turtle gently landed on his feet. Greedily he started to pick up the kernels which lay on the soil. And this greed caused him to forget Anancy's advice not to touch the stems of the plants. Thus those moved to and fro as if a strong breeze was blowing. Thus the rangers become aware of the presence of someone in the corn-field. They grabbed their guns, and hurried towards Anancy's friend. First, they could not spot him because Turtle was so small, but then they saw him.

"Halt!" They shouted. And "Stick 'em up!"

Brer Turtle was getting the shock of his life, and for nearly a minute he closed his eyes... (All of us do this when we're small, don't we? Because we used to think: If I can not see you, you can not see me neither).

The leading ranger grabbed Brer Turtle, and the others took his basket away from him.

"Hav' mercy, dear ranja-men!" arrested Brer Turtle

sighed. "Me nuh touch no ear of maize an me nuh t'ief not one kernel of maize wha nuh did lie pon de groun'. Please, lemme go!"

"Paragraph two hundred and forty-two of de Royal Lawbook seh: Whoevva tek way smaddie elks t'ings illegally shall be sentenced to five year ah prison wid hard labour!" The highest ranking Ranger pronounced seriously.

"But me ongly tek de half-rotten kernel-dem pon de ground!" Brer Turtle protested.

"De Judge have fi decide dat," the officer shouted. "An in dis-yah case yuh did t'ief suppen wha belong to de Crown. An fi dat yuh'll get capital punishment!"

But a crown can not own anything, the turtle was about to say, but he'd prefer to bite off his tongue than to tell this to the rangers. And he knew why: The Crown was The Right Honourable Lion, the King of the Animal Empire. And as a lion the crown is hungry. And as a hungry crown he craves for turtle-soup. Brer Turtle knew only too well how the Lion changed the laws all the while to be able to stuff his belly. One new law said: "It is forbidden to wear stripes. Only the police-force is allowed to wear red or blue seams on their pants. Every other citizen to be found wearing stripes will get the capital punishment!" (The Lion liked Zebra-meats!) A next law said: "It is forbidden to be the owner of long ears. Long-eared citizens will be killed!" And why? Because the Lion liked rabbit-meat and roasted hare. And as everybody knew only the Secret Service was allowed to have long ears. Paragraph 506, D/II/az, says: "It is forbidden by law to give calves a suck. Milk is the Crown's Property." And why? The Lion liked to drink cow's milk and to eat roast beef in red sauce.

Cool, cool down, the turtle told himself, while he was

walking to the King's Castle under heavy guard. And he started to whistle a tune. But the officer stopped him: "Whistling citizens cause noise-pollution. And an offence against the litter-act carries a sentence of two years in prison with hard labour."

But then Brer Turtle remembered Anancy's advice and started to sing: "Sammy plant piece ah corn dong ah gully...!"

This song brightened up the rangers, and they started to make dance-movements, and they sang along, and Brer Turtle's wonderful tenor came over them and straight into their hearts. Yes, as private men even police-men, bailiffs, warders, clerks of the court, judges, officers and courtiers have an heart! But only in private. Thus Brer Lion woke up from his lunch-nap, and he jumped to the window and roared: "Silence! Assume a pose! Officer, what does the report tell?"

"One prisoner and eight Royal Rangers on the way to the Royal Courthouse. A case of theft! Royal corn was stolen." The Officer shouted, the right hand at his temple, the eyes on the sky, the left hand ready to pull the gun.

"Do you order that we shoot the prisoner to death, Sire? As usual? Because he tried to escape?"

"No!" The Lion roared. "We give him a short shrift: Carry him straight to the Royal Chef! Me dead fi hungry fi turtle-soup. Stand down!"

"Yessir," the rangers shouted, and they drove the turtle with gun-butts and kicks directly into the Royal Kitchen.

The Royal Chef stood to attention: "I've taken delivery of culprit. Stand down, gentlemen!"

And even before all of the rangers had disappeared, the Royal Chef sharpened his long, big, pointed, sharp, sharp knife...

Brer Turtle cried a river. But the chef was unimpressed by that. But then Brer Turtle remembered Anancy's advice and started to sing: "If I had the wings of a dove, if I had the wings of a..."

"Dove!" the chef sang along enthusiastically. And they sang. And the Royal Chef moved his feet to the beat, and he threw away his knife and began to skank. And the Royal Chef started to cry a river as he was moved so much by the power of Brer Turtle's voice. And Brer Turtle crawled slowly backwards... and backwards... and backwards.

And the Royal Chef woke up as the turtle disappeared in the back of the Royal Kitchen Garden.

He was frightened. He knew too well that an escape of

a prisoner led to his watchdog's death. The chef looked around, took off his bloody apron, threw away the Royal Chef's hat and... ran away as fast as possible. Up to now, he is nowhere to be seen again.

When the King, Brer Lion heard about this, he cursed some badwords, and he swore never to employ a chef again. And from this day lions only eat raw meat.

And with a good conscience we can state that this was due to Anancy's advice to the turtle.

Jack Mandora, me nuh choose none.

14

Anancy and The Young Bull

Once upon a time there was a big and rough old bull who was married to seven cows and had lots of calves with them. Yes, this bull was no Christian. Christians only have one wife and consider themselves for sheep as Psalm 23 shows which reads: "The LORD IS MY SHEPHERD, I shall not want. He maketh me to lie down in a green pasture..."

Every day the bull got rougher and more intolerant and more violent. He boxed and beat and kicked his wives and children, and injured them quite often whenever he took them on his horns.

One day when the Bull went to the river to take a bath, his First Wife summoned a meeting.

"Nuttin cyaan gwan like dat again," she said. "Me's determine fi tek dat kinda behaviour no more. Yes, when fi we husban did young him did tender an polite. But now me cyaan tek him no more."

The other six cows moo'd loudly and nodded.

"Whoeva ah sow violence gwaan reap

violence," the First Wife continued. "Me propose seh we'll splash him wid kerosene an light him when him fass asleep. Whoeva support dat liff up de right front-foot!"

"No, no, no!" The youngest and most beautiful cow cried, who had married just recently because a calf was on the way.

"Gi him a chance fi better himself. We shoulda gi him a chance. In case him nuh change me propose fi expel him outa di district. Who wan fi second it liff up de lef frontfoot."

"Objection!" roared the Bull's Third Wife. "Me suggest fi attack him and kill him an leff him fa de John Crow-dem!" So every wife had a different proposal, and for the first time, the calves saw their mothers fussing. But only one calf, the son of the Second Wife dared open his mouth

and defend his father: "Apostle Paul seh: Ooman haffi shut up an obey!"

"Apostle Paul, me neck-back!" the Fourth Wife cried. "Firs' him kill off de Christian-dem, and den him turn inna one. Me nuh like nobaddy wha change him ways so often. Is we sheep or ram or lamb?"

"Yuh's right," the Fifth Wife bawled out, "pickney should be seen an' not be heard."

"Hear, hear!" All the cows were mooing. Then it got quiet.

Everybody racked their brain. Finally the Fourth Wife found a compromise: "We mek it perfectly clear to him seh him haffi pack him t'ings an move out!"

"Me second dat," the First Wife cried.

"We too," all the cows moo'd.

"An here, we must'n figat," the Fourth Wife said, watching the little bull-calf, "him can tek along dis yah feisty an' rude boy."

Even his own mother agreed because her young, powerful and cheeky son grieved her so much.

"But what can dem live on?" The Sixth Wife objected. "Oonoo know de man-dem. Dem cyaan get along widout de ooman-dem."

"Dat ah fi dem bizniz," the First Wife said. "De Ole Man hav' a big piece ah lan' inna de bush. Mek dem grab de lass an' farm."

Everybody agreed. When the Old Bull returned from the river to join the herd, his wives with kicks and horns forced him to pack his things and leave the area.

Early in the evening, father and son reached the overgrown piece of land in the bush. They were hungry and thirsty. The next river was a mile away, and the land the

bull had inherited from his grandfather was overgrown with cow-itch, thistles and thorns.

"Ah wha we's supposed fi do now?" The bull-calf asked.

The bull shrugged. "Soon me wi come up wid suppen."

Very tired, they walked to the river and filled their bellies with water. Then they lay down and fell asleep.

For breakfast there was nothing more than water too.

"Well, Ole Man, yuh come up wid suppen now?" The young Bull asked. "Me's a dead fi hungry."

"Is how yuh ah talk to yuh fadah?" The Big Bull roared. "Still, me got an idea before me drop asleep, Son. Yuh can read an 'rite, don't it?"

The Young Bull nodded. He used to go to school four days a week.

But because an old donkey was the teacher the Young

Bull used to play truant. Nevertheless he could read and write a little bit. And he could count up to twenty! He knew that he was not the brightest.

"Listen good-good," the Old Bull mildly said. "Yuh haffi write some posters an put dem up in all de hamlet and village dem. Write dat: Big piece ah land fi build! Best pay an' a big bonus! Ongly fi hardworking smaddies. Come an see John Bull, Lot 14, John Crow Mountains."

The Young Bull got pen and paper and started to write. Whenever a word was too difficult for him, his tongue could be seen in a corner of his muzzle. But then he remembered that his father had no money. So he ran to him with his posters and asked him what he meant by 'Pest Pay an Big Bonnos'.

The Old Bull grinned.

"Yes, me dear," he said roguishly, "me nuh tell yuh seh me wi come up wid suppen? De people dem shoulda glad fi get some work. So, why pay dem? De day gwaan come when millions ah unemployed smaddies work fi free. It ongly wan' ten t'ousand police an soljaman fi keep dem unda control. Listen: When de man-dem turn up fi build de land, we tell dem seh dem gwaan get a hundred dollar per acre. But unda one condition: Whoever scratch himself while him ah work him gwaan get nuttin..."

First the Young Bull did not understand him. But then he got it: The land was full of cow-itch, macca-bush and stinging nettles. Thus nobody would be able to suppress the urge to scratch himself. Yes, his father was sly fi true.

And as soon as the first poster was put up, lots of unemployed men turned up at Lot 14 in the John Crow Mountains. They were so desperate that they agreed to the conditions. The Old Bull only let two or three applicants work at the same time. He and his son watched them carefully. And no matter what the men did to protect themselves, sooner or later the stinging thistles caught them. The men put on rubber-gloves, leather-gloves or cloth-gloves; they put on two or three pants the same time, they tied rags around their calves, and they wore rubber-boots. But all this was in vain. They must scratch themselves! And then the Young and the Old Bull chased them away.

After two days, two acres of land were weeded and twenty-nine men got chased away without pay. Now less and less unemployed men turned up, and the Old Bull told the Young Bull to supervise the work, and left.

On the sixth day only two men turned up, on the seventh day nobody was looking for work anymore.

But on the eighth day a small, lively man turned up. He wore big cap, and he carried a very sharp machete under his arm. It was Anancy who had heard about the Bull's trickery and had made up his plan.

"Mawning, mawnin, proud, young and 'trong Mr. Bull Junior," he cried and bowed. "Me ah come fi do a first-class job."

"I guess so," the Young Bull replied licking his flank with his tongue. "Juss gwaan, and if yuh busy and finish de job before sun-down you'll get yuh pay and de good-good-bonus." Like father like son, Anancy told himself, and he wrapped up his hands, arms and his lower legs with rags of coarse cloth. Anancy spat into his palms and started to work in the unbearable heat. All the time, the Young Bull nibbled at the tender leaves of a tree. Now and then he cast a bored glance at Anancy.

Well, this one did his job skillfully and worked for more than half an hour without scratching himself. But all of a sudden a cow-itch caught him by his elbow. Anancy straightened himself. Now the Young Bull watched him carefully.

"Oh laaawks!" Anancy shouted. "What a handsome bull-calf yuh is! Juss look at this most charming white spot in your kneebend!"

"Which place?" The Young Bull asked him flattered.

"Right yah so," Anancy shouted, and he pointed at the bend of his elbow. Proudly the Bull peaked at the white spot in his knee-bend, and Anancy scratched his elbow unseen.

Cautiously he weeded again, but when he bent down after twenty minutes a macca-bush caught him at the chin. He glanced at the Young Bull who just stretched himself to nibble at a very juicy leaf on a bough.

"But what is this?" Anancy squealed of delight, and he danced on the spot. "Dis yah pretty, black mark 'pon yuh chin yuh mussi got from yuh madda-side!"

The young bull-calf tried to take a glance at the mark on his chin squinting terribly and did not look out for Anancy, who scratched his chin.

And so it went on the whole day long. Once in a while Anancy found 'a particularly pretty spot' in the Young Bull's fur and whenever the 'supervisor' inspected it proudly, Anancy was able to scratch himself without being caught.

At dusk Lot No. 14 was weeded out. When the Old Bull came, he found out that Anancy had done a wonderful job, 'without scratching himself', as the Young Bull reported.

"Yes, Daddy, him nevva scratch fi true."

The Old Bull suppressed his rage, disappeared behind an hedge, and dug out a bag with money his grandfather had buried in the ground before he died.

Anancy grabbed for the bag of money, he bowed politely, and disappeared. And as soon he had vanished, the Old Bull kicked his son terribly.

"Yuh nevva pay any attention, yuh rascal!" he roared.

The Young Bull tried to stay cool and contradicted gently: "But yes, Daddy, dat guy nevva scratch himself. Me nevva let him outa me sight. And, please, stop kicking me. Me too old to be treated like dat."

"Who ah rule, bwuoy? Me or yuh, yuh dutty bungle!" The Old Bull roared and gave him a taste of his horns. "Dat impossible seh one smaddy nuh haffi scratch himself when trillions of macca-dem an' thistle-dem an' cow-itch haffi weed-out!"

"But Daddy, me tell yuh awready seh yuh not supposed to kick, beat an jook lika dat. Soon me's a big bull. And deh's a law fi chile-abuse!" The Young Bull moo'd, very angry. "Dat man deh, him a special worker. Him immune to nettles an cow-itch."

"Immune, immune? Nobody immune atall-tall. An me can beat, kick an' jook yuh whenevva me feel like it. Me's fi yuh puppa. An yuh do-no-good of a watchman deserve some good-good licks and kicks!" And Old Bull took a run-up to take his son on his horns.

But the Young Bull just stepped aside, took a short, very fast run-up, took his father on his horns and with a powerful movement of the neck he threw him into the top of the tree at which he had been nibbling.

But then the Young Bull nearly fainted! What had he done? Yes, it was self-defence but even in self-defence one is not supposed to throw his own father into a tree-top.

He raised his mighty head and cast a glance at the tree-top. But he could not see his father.

And from this day fathers take good care not to beat up their sons after those have reached a certain age.

Anancy mek it.

And whenever you pass a fenced-up pasture and see a young bull nibbling the green grass and looking up once in a while and having a look at tree-tops, you can be sure that he is asking himself about the whereabouts of his father.

Don't tell him that a farmer has sold the old bull to a slaughter-house!

Jack Mandora, me nuh choose none.

15

Anancy and Jackass

One time Anancy was really lucky. His next-door neighbour got work abroad and asked Anancy to move into his house to take care of it. Anancy was very happy to leave his old shack with its rotten roof and to live in a big house with a pretty garden full of fruit-trees. And when he searched the wardrobe in the bedroom, he even found three suits which could fit him.

And so, every day Anancy sat in the rocking-chair on the verandah, smoked his pipe and enjoyed life. In high spirits, he watched what was going on on the premises across the road.

There was a beautiful girl living with her big brother. Her name was Georgia, and she belonged to that kind of people Anancy couldn't stand: She was stooshus and arrogant. Every day when Georgia's big brother left the yard to work in his fields, some young guys would turn up, lean on the fence, and try to have a word with this beauty. And whenever somebody told her that he loved her and wanted to marry her, Georgia watched him from head to toe, then got up to ridicule him so loud that everybody in the vicinity could hear it.

"Tell me who want a fat-so like yuh," she told a handsome, stout, young man. "Whe fi yuh wais' line deh?

Dat no wais' line, dat a tractor tyre 'pon de hips."

Or when the youth was small, she would say: "Who want a dwarf?" Or when someone had a beard: "Man, yuh've hair like monkey, Sah." And to a next one: "Yuh t'ink me wan' pickney for a man wid a broad nose like fi yuh one?" And to another one: "Yuh got bow-foot like cowboy an nuh even hav a horse?"

Georgia found fault with everyone. And whenever her big brother turned up, all these young men used to disappear. They were afraid of him. He was a huge man with hands as big as shovels.

Anancy got vexed with himself because he could not help but fall in love with her. Georgia was beautiful, and she was a hardworking girl. Yes, Anancy said to himself, the most important thing in life is to be healthy and to have a hardworking wife. So he decided to court Georgia. He dressed up with his friend's three-piece suit, put on his most colourful tie, cleaned his two-coloured suede-shoes, and put on his hat in the elegant style he had seen Brer Tiger with. Anancy looked into the mirror, and was very content with his looks, and a minute later, he entered the verandah of Georgia's house. She was sitting on a chair and made dollies with a folklore outfit she used to sell to tourists on the pier in the harbour.

Anancy bowed elegantly and said: "Good morning, beautiful Georgia. I'm Mr B.M.W. Mercedesbenz," imitating the heavy twang his cousin used to speak with after he came back from 'merica still poor, still dunce, without greenbacks and gold-teeth but with this accent (twang).

Georgia was deeply impressed by Anancy's behaviour.

Like nearly everybody in the country she preferred people and things that came from abroad. So she invited him to have a seat, asked him whether he wanted a drink, and got up. Anancy sank in the chair casually, and asked for a glass of champagne or whisky. Georgia was so impressed that she was left speechless. She had to swallow hard, and answered in a quivering voice: "Sorry, Sah, bot we nuh got dat. Wha' bout a white rum wid coconut-wata?"

"It won't bother me, Beautiful," Anancy replied, and

asked her to sit back. And they had a good chat until it was getting dark. Georgia was convinced that she had fallen in love with Mr. Mercedesbenz undyingly. But all of a sudden, her brother came back from his fields. He used to guard his sister jealously, and some years ago he had promised his mother on her deathbed that Georgia only should marry a decent and very rich man. Now, as he got nearer to the verandah, and saw this elegantly clad man, he thought that this guy could be Georgia's Prince Charming. Politely he said "Howdie!" But as soon as he reached the last step leading to the verandah, he identified Anancy, and got vexed.

"Georgia!" he shouted, "How often me tell yuh not fi chat wid stranjas. Dat man deh ah de biggest jinnal an' tricksta widin hunnerd miles!"

And he lifted his machete and shouted: "Dat a real feistiness! Yuh come yah inna disguise an court fi me sista! Me gi' yuh one minute fi run 'way, yuh... trickster!"

Anancy jumped up, and raised his hat slightly, and ran around Georgia's brother, boiling with rage – and disappeared only too glad not to be beaten.

As he crossed the road in a hurry, he saw Brer Jackass who had seen and heard what happened on the verandah and laughing: "He-haw! He-haw! Heeeeee-haw!"

Abruptly Anancy came to a standstill. He felt ashamed. He was vexed that a stupid donkey was laughing at him. So Anancy put on a false smile, and said in his sweetest voice:

"Ah wha yuh laugh 'bout, Brer Jackass?"

The donkey wiped his eyes and answered: "Well, Anancy, how come you could t'ink seh Georgia rate yuh? She even ridicule all dese handsome an rich smaddies wha wan' fi marry har."

Anancy put on a sad face and said, after a while: "Yuh's right, Brer Jackass, smaddy like me got no chance wid har. If I did big an' 'trong like yuh..."

"Ah true?" Brer Jackass asked.

"True, true! Yuh's a jackass, yuh donkey," Anancy answered. "Yuh nuh got no yeyes? Yuh nevva see seh Georgia love yuh bad-bad? She only too shy fi tell yuh. An she a deestant gal."

Brer Jackass was flabbergasted.

"Yuh t'ink seh me shoulda propose to har?"

"Yeah, man. What else, yuh Jackass? She de most beautiful an most hardworking gal around. Mek me tell yuh suppen: When yuh go ah dance nex' weekend again, put on you bes' an dance wid har, and de nex mawnin yuh carry har straight to a parson or a justice of the peace."

"Ah-Ah-Ah-Anancy," stammered Brer Jackass, "yuh really is a good, good frien'! Tanks fi de advice! Friday coming me'll go to a place whe dem lease tuxedos. An Saturday night me gwaan check Georgia. Gals like har haffi be taken by storm."

"Ah wha me did tell yuh?" Anancy replied, and turned his face to the side to hide his dirty grin.

The following Saturday, Georgia's brother bathed with water from the rain-barrel. Georgia put on her Sunday's best and called from the kitchen-window: "Likkle more. Me gone ah church right now."

Her brother nodded and continued to brush his fingers.

But instead of going to church, Georgia ran to her best friend's house. The girls had a good chat, they ate a late supper, and about ten o'clock they walked to the dancehall. It was very dark inside. After a while the girls noticed a

good looking, strong, big man in a tuxedo, sitting on a stool at the bar. He felt their eyes on his back, and turned around. Then he jumped up and asked Georgia for a dance. At first she played coy, but after he had ordered an expensive long drink for her and after they had a nice, little chat she was very impressed by the stranger. Those broad shoulders! Those long and muscular thighs and legs! Those dark, glowing eyes with their long lashes! (Well, yes, his ears were a bit long. But what? Well, yes, his mouth was a bit big... But what he says! And how he says something! Ejejej!) And then they – danced. And within minutes, the other dancers left the dance floor to watch them, to clap hands and to whistle and to cheer them.

And whenever the selector made a pause, the elegant stranger led Georgia to the counter and ordered a cocktail and pushed a man from his bar-stool as he said, "got no manners! Yuh haffi offer yuh seat to a lady, yuh Raggamuffin!" Around midnight, Georgia whispered: "Yes, but yes," when Brer Jackass asked her to become his wife.

And early the next morning, the two of them went to a Justice of the Peace and got married. Can you imagine Georgia's disappointment when they reached the stable the donkey lived in? He had promised her a big villa with a huge yard and helpers and gardeners and chauffeurs and undescribable luxuries! Brer Jackass tore Georgia's beautiful dress off her body and threw some rags to her to get dressed in. And he gave her a broom, and ordered to clean the stable immediately. Because of her shock and disappointment, Georgia was unable to move. Then the jackass bit her shoulder and turned around and fired his back feet at her and gave her some terrible kicks. He did not know better: He had seen his father and grand-father treating their wives like that. And when Georgia's brother turned up to free her out of this miserable marriage, Brer Jackass kicked and bit him so bad that he had to be taken to the hospital.

And each and every year Georgia delivered a baby, and each and every year Brer Jackass got more brutal, beating and kicking wife and children and wasting his hard-earned money in bars.

And from that day, girls and women who are looking for their Prince Charmings in dancehalls and bamboo-lawns only get jackasses as husbands.

Anancy mek it.

16

Anancy and The Bull's Tongue

Once upon a time Anancy had to pack his things and leave his village as some people were getting serious and wanted back the money Anancy had borrowed from them. After two days he reached a kingdom he had heard about a lot. He rented a tiny shack and looked for people he could trick.

Soon he understood that in the woodlands near to the capital of the kingdom, a huge bull was living and haunting the people.

The people in the roads and in bars told all kind of terrible stories about it. The bull had killed several hunters already who had gone into the woodlands to kill him.

So the King of the country had promised to marry off his daughter to anyone who was able to kill the bull. And with the daughter came half of the kingdom as a dowry. As a proof that the hunter had killed the bull he had to cut out the bull's tongue, which was of pure gold.

Anancy took a seat in his rocking-chair under a tamarind tree, lighted his pipe and racked his brain. Suddenly he jumped up and ran to the King's Palace. Before working on a plan how to kill the bull, he had to see the princess. He did not trust the King. Maybe the King's daughter was ugly. Or she was stubborn. Or she was vain and cantankerous. Or she was too old. Or she was skilled in martial arts or boxing. No, Anancy wanted to be sure that his future wife would harmonize with him, he was quite sure that would get the bull's tongue.

In front of the King's Palace was a square, which was used as a market on weekends.

Anancy squatted down on his heels beside a fat, old market woman who sold pineapples, papayas and mangoes, and he asked her about the virtues and vices of the princess. Yes, concerning women, Anancy did not ask teachers, professors, tax-office clerks or parsons. He rated the common sense of people from the country. You could imagine how surprised Anancy was getting, when the old woman counted the princess' virtues on the fingers of her hands. Was he to believe this lady the princess was intelligent, independent-minded, beautiful, not vain, not interested in designer-clothes or jewellery. Yes, according to the higgler, the princess was even hard-working, caring, sweet, a friend of common people, good to children, tender, charitable...

"An no vice atall-tall?" Anancy disrupted the old lady after ten minutes. She watched him carefully.

"It depen' wha you tek fi vice or virtue," she said finally. "Me know whole heap a man-dem wha nevva rate intelligence, independence and pride inna woman."

Anancy frowned, and from then on he watched the big gate of the palace to see when the princess would come out to shop.

The old higgler had told him that the Princess herself did the shopping for the Royal Kitchen, and that the higglers in the market loved her so much that they gave her the best fruits, vegetables and the best meats, and always – a brawta. Suddenly the gate opened, and Anancy saw a dozen beautiful, young women approaching, all of them clad simply and clean. Nobody had to tell him who the Princess was. Seeing her he fell in love at first sight. Anancy was daydreaming. Yes, this was the woman of his life! He jumped up, he expressed his thanks to the old higgler, and he ran straight to his son Tucuma's yard. Yes, Anancy had children in every parish, every county, every kingdom around. The women just loved him. But up to now he did not find any one he would like to marry.

Tucuma was tall and handsome, but a little bit shy. Anancy liked him, and Tucuma liked his father despite the fact that Anancy never sent maintenance-money to his mother and did not help him with his education. But time longer than rope; and now Anancy could make up for it.

Tucuma was just about to boil coconut-oil and was glad to see his father in a healthy and jolly state.

"Tell me suppen, bwuoy," Anancy said after a while – forgetting that his son was far taller than he, "don't yuh feel like killing de bull wid de golden tongue?"

"Naaaah," Tucuma answered.

"Why not?" Anancy asked.

"Well, me did catch all kinda dangerous animals awready," Tucuma said, "Me did kill lion, tiger, panther, leopard, wile boar, an' elephant-bull but dis yah bull too dangerous. Fi me taste, too much hunter-dem did lose dem lives when dem did try fi catch de bull."

"Well, son, sit dong an listen!"

They took a seat on a tree-trunk, and while they smoked a big pipe, Anancy told Tucuma his plan how to catch the bull without endangering himself.

Well, the next morning Tucuma entered a hardware store and bought what Anancy told him to buy. After that, he walked to the woodlands. Having reached the river, he filled the big, red bag he had bought, with wet sand and gravel, and dragged it to the clearing in the woods where Anancy had seen fresh traces of the bull's hooves. Then he climbed a big tree, sat down on a strong bough and lifted up the bag with a strong rope. He estimated the distance between the forest soil and the bough he was sitting on. He cut the rope accordingly. Now, he settled down comfortably on the bough with his back against the trunk, and balanced the heavy, big, red bag with his left hand.

It was getting dark when he saw the bull in the clearing. And what a bull this was! It was huge and muscular, it's neck was swollen, it looked very fast, nervous and cautious... It's eyes were red, and foam dripped from it's snout.

Very slowly and carefully, Tucuma let down the bag from the bough till it swang over the forest soil. The bull saw the swinging, red bag. It heaved and started running!

Never before had Tucuma ever seen such a fast bull. The bull lowered it's head, ran full speed against the dangling bag to take it on its horns and...collapsed!

"Yes, yes, yes!" Tucuma shouted.

The bull shook it's head like a groggy boxer. The bull tried to get up. It's knees were shaking. It was looking towards Tucuma on the bough. That very moment, Tucuma threw the rope with it's sling around the bull's neck and tightened it like a hangman's noose. The half-fainted bull applied it's weight against it. But the more it pressed, the more the sling choked it. With a last, terribly loud "Mooooo!" it trembled and fell. It was dead!

Tucuma stayed on the bough until he was sure that the bull was really dead and did not breathe anymore.

With trembling knees Anancy's big son climbed down the tree trunk, took the machete out of it's sheath, and cut off the huge animal's head with the golden tongue in its mouth.

Joyfully whistling, he went home. There a good dinner of stew-peas was waiting on him.

"Well, wha me did tell yuh?" Anancy said. They ate slowly and in peace, enjoying the good food. They finished their dinner with a cup of coffee and a pipe.

"Well, bwoysie," Anancy finally said, "you'll sell de tongue to the Indian jeweller inna de nex kingdom' capital an send your nex-door neighbour dem to dat clearing an mek dem share de bull's meat. An me'll go to de King's Palace tomorrow mawnin fi get de reward."

"Me wish yuh all de bes," Tucuma grunted. He was not too fond of the idea of getting a distinguished stepmother as he had trouble enough already with his own mother and his eight siblings.

Early next morning, Anancy was on the way to the King's Palace. When the guards saw this small, shabbily clad guy with the bull's horns sticking out of the knapsack he carried, they were flabbergasted. But then all of them shouted "Hurrah!", and they carried Anancy on their shoulders to the King.

The King was so happy and surprised, that he did not bother to have a look at the golden tongue in the bull's mouth. He just ordered to start the wedding celebrations immediately. Anancy got his velvet wedding-uniform with golden buttons, a general was his bestman; and the princess in her bridal dress was as beautiful as the sunrise over the Caribbean. Her bridesmaid was an admiral's daughter. And before you could wink your eye, the two were married. Everyone was invited to the merrymaking; rich and poor, young and old, black and white. There was the most delicious food for everybody. And the King's Royal Band was playing some hot music.

The King asked Anancy to take his wife by the hand and to start the dance. Anancy was so happy, he thought he lived in a dream. While Anancy danced with the princess, the officer of the Royal Guard got the idea to peep into the bull's mouth. He asked the Royal Chef to lend him a big knife to cut out the tongue. But he looked and looked – and did not see any tongue!

"Your Majesty," he shouted with sweat on his brow, "this man is a swindler... a fraud, a...crook, a... trickster!"

He pointed to Anancy. "There is no tongue at all in the bull's mouth," the officer declared, now a little calmer. "It looks as if there was no tongue or this... conman has cut it out and stolen it."

The King nearly got an heart-attack. He lifted his arm and pointed to Anancy.

"Arrest this marriage impostor! Right now," he shouted. The Royal Guard ran toward Anancy and his new wife. But the princess was faster than them. She grabbed her new husband's hand and ran with him to their bedroom. But the soldiers were faster than they were. The princess tried to slam the door, but the officer grabbed the door-handle and forced the door open. The princess collapsed and cried and cursed her father.

"Finally I got a nice husband and not a stiff nobleman," she sobbed, "and now my wicked father wants to kill him!"

Meanwhile Anancy racked his brain: Should he hide under the bed? In the walk-in closet or in the bathrooms? Then he remembered his old magic: He turned into a big spider

and hurriedly climbed up the wall. In a corner of the ceiling he started to weave his spider-net. The soldiers could not arrest him again. The officer posted a guard consisting of seven heavily armed soldiers in front of the bedroom-door: Anancy had no chance to escape.

Thus the princess started to catch flies, grasshoppers, and mosquitoes for her husband to feed him. In the long run she taught him to catch them himself. From that day, spiders are very useful insects. And you and me know that whatever happens we never, ever will trouble a spider: It catches mosquitoes and other insects.

Anancy mek it.

Jack Mandora, me nuh choose none.

(PS: I never understood how Anancy could escape from the bedroom. But he did. And I'm only too glad about it. Aren't you too?)

17

Anancy and Peel-Head Fowl

Once upon a time - but this is really long, long time ago - the country had a very good Minister of Agriculture. He had a good plan to help the farmers. These were barely able to earn a decent living. So the Minister decided to help the farmers with loans, credits and outreach officers who could give advice what to plant and when to plant, and to earn good money by growing vegetables and fruits for export.

Well, Anancy stands at the gate of his yard, and he watches the farmers passing by with their donkeys. The square-cornered baskets made of palm-thatch the farmers used to call bankras are full of produce. The farmers are smiling. For the first time they are getting good money for their hard-hard work. Anancy is getting envious...

And he lies down in his hammock, lights his pipe and racks his brain how to get vegetables and foodstuff, too, which he could bring to the Export Board. The Board has built big cooling - houses to store the foodstuff, to process and to export it. Anancy can see with his own eyes that even lazy farmers are busy now planting vegetables and reaping fruits, digging yams, cocos and dasheens. Yes, Anancy tells himself, the times are good to farmers. Then he gets an idea.

On Saturday evening Anancy calls all the farmers to the village square.

"Genklemen," he cries, "me did notice seh de manners inna de distric' dem ah get wos' and wossera. Wha cause i'? People getting greedy. Greedy like de people-dem a foreign. An' why? Causen dem mek money nowadays. Nuttin wrong wid mekin' money! No, no! But me aks ooonoo wedda dat awright when bad mannerism tek ova? Dat people start disrespec' each odda? No! Dat de reason why me did call dis yah meetin'. All a we shoulda mek a resolution: Whoevva diss sistren an' breddren, frien' an' foe, nex-door neighbour an' ole people haffi pay a fine. Whoevva guilty ah dissin a nex person shoulda gi' de produce him carry wid him to de person wha got diss'!"

The older farmers nod. They had the same experience. Young farmers have started laughing at people who can not work as hard as they can. Therefore the majority of the people in the square decide to make this rule: "Whoever disrespects hard working people has to compensate the disrespected person with the contents of the baskets their donkeys are carrying or the content of the basket the culprit carries on top of his head!"

Early next morning, the sun is seeing something it has never seen before so early: Anancy is working with hoe and machete! Yes, Anancy is working hard. He is standing on top of a boulder beside the road which leads to the farmland, his hoe in his two hands trying to dig holes into the boulder....

Some minutes later Brer Jackass is passing by. The bankras on his back are full of yams. Jackass has got up before dawn to work, and now he is carrying his produce to the Export Board. Seeing Anancy on top of the boulder sweating and digging, Brer Jackass can not say a word.

"Ah wha yuh ah do, Anancy," Jackass brays after a while.

"Yuh nuh see: Me ah dig hole fi plant yams, Brer Jackass," Anancy cries and wipes his forehead.

Now Jackass has to start laughing: "But what is this?" he cries. "One evva see smaddy wha plant yams pon a boulder?" And he laughs and laughs, he wipes laughing tears from his eyes. "Eeee-ah! Eee-ah!" He laughs.

"'top dat!" Anancy shouts. "Yuh nuh see see yuh ah diss me? Now yuh haffy pay de fine! Gimme fi yuh yams right now!"

Brer Jackass lowers his head. He feels shame. He has commited the crime to laugh at a hard working person. Thus he hands over his two baskets which are filled with yams to Anancy.

As soon as Brer Jackass is our of sight, Anancy starts to smile: His plan is working! He can cheat hard-working people out of their produce!

A quarter of an hour later, Brer Ramgoat is passing by. He carries a heavy load of plantains on his head - and seeing Anancy he stops in his tracks.

"But see-yah!" Ramgoat cries. "What a fool-fool! Yuh mussi be a dunce, Anancy. Yuh evva see smaddy wha try fi plant suppen pon top ah boulders?"

Anancy watches him sternly. "Yams me ah plant," he says.

"Yams cyaan grow pon boulder, sah," Brer Ramgoat laughs. "Yuh's an eediot, Anancy!"

"Got yuh!" Anancy cries. "How yuh dare diss me, sah? Dat ah out-a-order! Yuh haffi pay de fine right now."

Ramgoat is feeling shame now: Yes, he has disrespected Anancy. And this is not right. He hands over his plantains to Anancy, and walks off slowly.

Five minutes later, the biggest farmer in the district is passing by. He is Mr. Miller, a white man, who owns more than one hundred acres of land. He is riding on horseback and is leading three donkeys on a tight rein.

Having seen Anancy Mr. Miller shouts: "Cooo-yah, but what is this? Ah wha yuh a do, Anancy? Ah wha yuh a do so early ah mawnin' awready?"

"Yuh nuh see, Mr. Miller, me ah dig yam-bank right yah so," Anancy answers.

"Yam bank on top ah de boulder, Anancy? Yuh mussi crazy!"

Anancy straightens up himself. "Long time me know yuh, Backra, but me nevva know seh yuh ah diss hard-working people. Yuh nevva know de new law?"

Mr. Miller lowers his head in shame.

"Yuh's right, Anancy, me sorry. Me sorry, me say!"

"Sorry, sah? Yuh's not sorry at all-tall! Now, yuh haffi pay me de fine! Gimme fi yuh produce right now! Yuh haffi stick to de same law like evvrybuddy elks. De Backra-days ova, Sir!"

Mr. Miller is deeply ashamed, and he dismounts from his horse, and he unloads six heavy baskets full of bananas, plantains, cucumbers, cho-chos and dasheen, bids Anancy a farewell and leaves.

Anancy rubs his bands: He even could trick the richest and most powerful man in the district. His plan is wonderful.

In the meantime, the farmers who got tricked by Anancy are gathering in the village-square and tell each other what they have experienced. Now they find out that Anancy only has used his brain which is full of tricks. They don't know what to do. At the moment the crowd is dispersing, Sister Peel-Head Fowl passes by.

"Wha happen?" She cackles.

The farmers tell her what has happened to them.

"Breddren," Sister Peel-Head Fowl cackles, "we shoulda know seh suppen strange gwaan happen whenevva dis yah ginnal name Anancy propose a new rule or law. Me gwaan teach him a lesson!"

"Yuh, Sister?" The farmers wonder.

"Yes, me," Peel-Head Fowl answers humbly, and she walks to her yard to trick the trickster.

Ten minutes later Sister Peel-Head Fowl is passing Anancy. He still is standing on the boulder, working hard.

Peel-Head-Fowl pretends not to see him.

"Good mawnin, Sister Peel-Head Fowl," Anancy cries, wiping sweat from his face. "Ah whe yuh ah go?"

"Mawnin, Anancy, sah," Peel-Head Fowl answers politely. "Well man, deh's a dance tonight inna de Bamboo Lawn. An me haffi godeh. Me done buy some bashment-clothes awready, an now me's on me way to de beauty-saloon. Me gwaan be de mos' stylish ooman inna de dance. Miss Lena inna de beauty-saloon haffi jerry-curl me hair an put some braids inna me hair. An den, Anancy," she cries with joy, "an den she haffi dye fi me owna hair an de braids inna green, gold an' red. Yes, man, me gwaan be de mos' beautiful gal inna de bashment!"

"Yuh!" Anancy cries.

"Yes, man, me!" Peel-Head Fowl proudly answers.

"But me nevva see smaddy wha have no hair pon de head, not a single hair, an go ah beauty-saloon fi prettify de hairstyle!" Anancy shakes with laughter.

"Catch yuh!" Sister Peel-Head Fowl cackles sombrely. "Yuh's a wokless smaddy, Anancy, yuh diss me bad-bad!"

Anancy stops laughing. With wide open eyes he watches the only person who could trick him. He feels shame. He lowers his head, and with tears in his eyes he is handing over all the produce he has got from the farmers to Peel-Head Fowl. And for the next ten years she is the only person who was able to trick the most notorious trickster in history.

Jack Mandora, me nuh choose none.

18

Anancy and Jaguar

For some years now Anancy had been married to Aso, a King's daughter, and it was wonderful how she mastered life. She was born with a golden spoon in her mouth, and now she experienced – like most people in the country – poverty, arrogant officers in government offices, a violent police-force, hunger, sickness, and sometimes homelessness too.

Anancy loved his princess very much, even though sometimes she had to rough him up because of his dislike of hard work. Thus the whole family very often was hungry. But Aso never complained.

She worked hard and managed the money, she sent the children to school, and she did not mind washing other people's clothes or to cook for them or to babysit.

Anancy was lying in his hammock. It was a sunny Sunday. There came his wife and overturned his hammock. Bapps! He dropped out.

"How yuh mean seh teday a Sunday? We hungry, man."

Anancy's two little boys liked that. They climbed on their father's back because they remembered too well how Anancy tricked Tiger by riding on him. And thus they always want to play with their father.

But now Aso clapped her hands.

"No more play-play," she cried.

"Oh no!" Anancy and his sons bawled out. And: "It ah Sunday teday," they call.

"On a Sunday all ah we still can go ah bush an' collect fruits an berries," the mother decided.

Then everybody jumped up with laughter, and they ran to the house, grabbed crocus-bags and baskets, and in not even five minutes everybody was ready to walk to the bush.

There they picked Seville oranges and cherries and June-plums, and filled their bellies, bags and baskets. And everybody was excited when Anancy discovered jimbelins near to a fence. Aso would stew them. And so they picked and picked, and they moved deeper and deeper into the woodland.

Suddenly they saw a beautiful villa in a clearing!

Aso was frightened and put her hands in front of her mouth.

Anancy scratched his head. The children watched the villa with mouths wide open.

"Lawwwwdamassi," Anancy said," ah who coulda mek such a beautiful house deep-deep inna de woodlan?"

"Maybe de witch outa de fairy-tale?" his youngest son said.

"Nuh witch nuh deh inna real life!" the other children cried.

"Shhhhh!" Anancy said, and everybody became dead-silent.

Anancy and his wife watched each other. Then Anancy cleared his throat and shouted: "Anybody home? Hole de dog!"

No answer.

Now Aso whispered into Anancy's ear. He whispered back, and Aso took the children by their hands, and they hid behind a big bush while Anancy tiptoed towards the villa. He looked through a high window. Nobody was to be seen. Anancy tiptoed to the front door. It was open... Hm.

Anancy plucked up his courage and entered the house. He tiptoed through the hall, opened a mahogany-door and crept into the room. It was the dining-room. Cautiously,

Anancy searched the whole villa, but only when he reached the master-bedroom he found out who was living in the house. On a bedside-table Anancy noticed a fashion-magazine for she-jaguars...

"Brer Jaguar an him wife," Anancy murmured. "But dem gone out. Hm."

Having opened the bedroom-window he beckoned to Aso and the children gesturing to keep silent. Silently they got nearer, and Anancy showed them the way to the kitchen.

There he opened a huge deep-freezer and all of them couldn't say a word: The freezer was full of antilope-filets, pig quarters, T-bone-steaks, chickens, turkeys, and other kinds of meat! Not even in a butcher's shop or in the market, Anancy's family had seen so much meat kind. And it was a long time now that they had been in a butcher's shop: Anancy and his wife were so poor that for months they could not afford to buy meat.

"I never dreamed that it would come to this," Aso said and digged into the deep-freezer to get out a juicy cut of beef. "Me as a big oman wha t'ief a nobleman like Brer Jaguar!" And she laughed.

Then she went into the kitchen to season up the meat and to prepare the dinner. In the meantime Anancy and his children set the table, mixed a jarful of lime-ade, used the mattresses as a trampoline, and watched the pictures in a fashion-magazine called "For you: *The Magazine For The Elegant Jaguar-Lady*," and they laughed.

After a while they heard Aso calling: "Dinner ready!" They washed their hands and ran down the steps to the first floor. Suddenly Anancy had to sneeze. He raised his head and held his nose – and he nearly dropped dead:

Looking through the window he saw Brer Jaguar and his wife as they dragged a cow they had hunted and killed, towards the house! Fast like lightning Anancy ran into the kitchen and whispered into Aso's ear. She got pale and nodded.

"Sit dong, sit dong, dinnertime now!" Anancy shouted full force.

The children ran into the dining-room and took their seats around the huge table with its expensive table-cloth. Anancy stopped in the door-frame for a moment, and in the corner of his eye he saw Brer Jaguar and his wife looking through the window of the dining-room. The children bawled out! Fast like lightning Anancy jumped over to his eldest son, snatched him, and gave him a sound spanking!

In that moment Aso turned up with the tray of food. The son bawled murder.

"Ah wha yuh beat him fah, Anancy?" Aso shouted. "Ah wha him ah do?"

"Imagine, wife, dat likkle nuisance ah choosey bout de food! Him ah seh him nuh want beef wid mash pitatoe. Roast' jaguar-meat him want! But not outa tin. Fresh jaguar-meat him want. An me is sick'n' tiad fi hunt jaguar-dem day in an' day out. An me's even more tiad fi nyam jaguar-meat! Jaguar-fillet, jaguar-mince, jaguar-tongue inna wine-gravy, jaguar-kidney, jaguar-liver...! Me sick n' tiad ah alla dat jaguar-meat, tiad, tiad, tiad!"

Aso dropped the gravy-bowl. The children cried murder. Anancy whipped the boy with his belt, and Aso encouraged him to do it, and she shouted: "Yes, man, gi' him a good spanking! Me is sick'n'tiad too fi cook jaguar-meat each and ebbry day. Me nebba gone a cooking-school juss fi cook ongly one kinda meat! Beat him, Anancy, beat him good-good!"

"Fi yuh son!" Anancy shouted.

"No, fi yuh son dat!" Aso yelled back.

And in the corner of his eye Anancy saw how Brer Jaguar

and his wife watched each other frightened, and then he saw how they ran through the front-yard as if the leggo-beast was chasing them. In five seconds Brer Jaguar and his wife disappeared in the darkness of the woodland.

From that day, no jaguar is living in a villa anymore. And whenever you see a jaguar in the jungle or in the zoo you'll find him resting on a branch of a big tree and dozing.

Anancy mek it.

AFTERWORD

The protagonist of our stories - by far the most popular ones in the Caribbean - Anancy, originally was a minor sub-god in the realm of the gods of the Ashantis, the famous, big and bellicose people of Ghana, Africa. *Kwaku* (born on Wednesday) *Ananse* (spider) was the spider-god, a being in human shape who could turn into a spider whenever he was faced with dangerous situations.

To characterise this minor god, the *Dictionary of Jamaican English* says: "Anancy, the spider, pits his cunning (usually with success) against superior strength. He also symbolises greed and envy."

In one word: Anancy is a trickster-god. This kind of minor god was common in other religions worldwide. The German realm of gods had *Loki*, the Greek had *Hermes* (the God of thieves and businessmen), the Polynesian had *Maui*, the Japanese had *Kitsune, the Fox*, and the Amerindian in the Southwest of the U.S.A. had the *Coyote*.

Conditioned by the unbelieveable cruelties the slaves in the Caribbean had to suffer, the relatively harmless, mythological stories about Kwaku Ananse was turned into more brutal and more wicked ones. Fairy tales and myths worldwide were conditioned

125

by social realities, and they adapt to them.

The little, always hungry, sly work-dodger, Anancy the Trickster, bamboozles everybody, the Lion and the Tiger, the Giant Yellow Snake and the Elephant. Thus it is only too understandable how Anancy became a popular figure of identification for the slaves and their children and greatgrand-children. He embodies the victory of wit, of imagination, and the presence of mind over the brute force of the great and mighty ones.

There are many who call Anancy the Real National Hero and Patron Saint of Jamaica. The highbrow and upper middle-classes were and still are waging an ideological war against *Anancyism*: As long as Anancy determines the people's character, they say a Third World country would be unable to turn into a developed one.

In a certain way Anancy-stories are similar to stories about Till Eulenspiegel and Reineke Fox in Germany, Nasreddin in Turkey, Brer Rabbit in the (Black) U.S.A. and Compère Lapin in the French Creole speaking isles of the Caribbean.

But Anancy is more than that, he is of godly origins, and thus the stories contain a part of cosmology, a mythic-poetical interpretation of the world. Simply expressed: Anancy was in the end, responsible for the small changes of creation. *"Anancy mek it!"* that pigs have a snout,that wasps don't have teeth but a sting, that cats are hunting mice and rats, that chicken eat cockroaches, that mongooses kill chickens, that tigers in spite of their strength hide in the jungle, that citizens don't have to buy wedding-presents for their kings, presidents and prime-ministers, that each and everybody has at least a little bit of common sense, etc. etc. All this and more *Anancy mek it.*

M.G. "Monk" Lewis was the first person to collect Anancy-stories and to write them down (*Journal of a Westindian Proprietor,* 1734). A beautiful collection of songs and Anancy-stories was put together by Walter Jekyll (Folklore Publications, 1907); and Martha Warren Beckwith edited a collection of Anancy-stories in 1924 in which music taped and transcribed by Helen Roberts is to be found (*American Folklore Society, G.E. Stechert & Co.*). For her doctor's thesis Laura Tanna in 1985 published *Jamaica Folk Tales and Oral History*. She collected stories from April 1973 till October 1974 in hamlets, villages and towns all over Jamaica. She found the most important story-tellers, audiotaped and filmed their performances, and transcribed them. In her book we find the very African heritage of oral traditions. These documents of an oral based culture are now available, as a book, audio and video cassettes (*Institute of Jamaica Publications Ltd.*).

The most beautiful and most popular versions of Anancy-stories were told by Jamaica's Cultural Ambassadress, Louise Bennett, affectionately called *Miss Lou*. (Federal Records, FRM-129).

In the thirties, as a teenager, Miss Lou used to write poems in Patois. Up to now, the ruling classes in Jamaica despise the mother-tongue of the island's citizens, and unfortunately this language is not taught in the schools. Thus the people "learn to read a language they do not speak and cannot write a language which they speak daily."

Miss Lou was not only an actress, a broadcaster, and a star in her own TV-show, she did not only write poems and witty short-stories. Miss Lou up to now is one of Jamaica's greatest (amateur) anthropologists and linguists. She made the common Jamaicans proud of their heritage, of their traditions, their music, their witty language, their...roots!

Her Anancy-stories stay as near as possible to their oral tradition, we only miss her wonderful ways to perform – but recently a very good video was taped and is for sale now, as Jamaicans use to say: "Whenever an old person dies it's like a town-library is getting burnt down."

127

But whoever thinks that in Miss Lou's versions we've got the last ones to be enshrined in a book - and cannot be altered anymore, is dead wrong. Contrary to countries with a culture of script, e.g. Germany with the fairy-tales collected and written down by the Brothers Grimm, every night in Jamaica thousands of grannies, aunties and (far less) fathers, mothers and nurses are telling Anancy-stories to the children. The Institute of Jamaica and the Festival Organisation invite entries for a competition for story-tellers, and they store the best ones in a *"Memory Bank"*.

As a professional writer I'm jealous of the original story-tellers with their live-performances. Thus I tried to write new versions of Anancy-stories. Like story-tellers in West and North Africa, the Middle East and in the Caribbean, I stick to a short ("rump") version of a story which, e.g., in Martha Beckwith's collection just takes half a page - and then I elaborate on it. This is the job of a writer.

As a nationalized, not a born, Jamaican I have tried to continue in the oral tradition I love, but I have now done what the English writer Peggy Appiah did with her ashanti husband's stories. (*The Stories of an Ashanti Father*, written by Peggy Appiah, André Deutsch, London 1967).

Having told Anancy-stories to my Jamaican-born children nearly every night, I started to write them down and elaborate on them even more.

Walter Benjamin once wrote:

"At the narration the trace of the narrator is as sticking as the trace of the potter's hand is sticking at the bowl of clay," and I do hope that I – here and there – as a narrator am creating as Benjamin said, "the shape in which the righteous man is meeting himself."

Anancy-stories never ever will be written to an end, and will never ever get a definitive shape – as for example Grimm's Fairy

Tales. They are however, a living ingredient of an everlasting, never ending culture of a people. Maybe then, the stories in this book can stimulate the reader and his young listeners at bedtime to start to develop and tell their own Anancy-stories. Like, "Why the banana is bent?" *Anancy mek it...* Or they are stimulated to change well-known bedtime-stories according to there taste. A good book is a stimulation of imagination and mind.

Reading or listening, our imaginations start floating, our horizon is enlarged; indeed recreation and enlightenment should join together.

Peter-Paul Zahl

Rose Hill, Long Bay, Portland,
September 2001

ABOUT THE AUTHOR

Peter-Paul Zahl, a son of a publisher for childrens' books, was born in Germany in 1944. He has lived in Jamaica since 1985 and has six children and three stepchildren in five countries.

He writes novels, poetry, essays and plays for theatre and radio. He is a qualified printer and theatre-director. His first publication was in 1968 and since then his books have been published in Germany, Greece, France, Denmark, the Netherlands and Japan.

His first childrens' book was published in 1998. Zahl received the Literature Award of the Free and Hansetown of Bremen, Germany, in 1980 and the 1994 the Glauser Award for the best mystery novel.

A second book with Anancy Stories "for people from seven to one hundred and ten", ANANCY THE TRICKSTER, will be published in the near future.

LMH Publishing also plans to publish Zahl's Reggae Mysteries, a series of crime-novels situated in Jamaica.

Printed in the United States
28817LVS00005B/433-558